The Western Alienation Merit Badge

D1466804

Also by Nancy Jo Cullen

Fiction
Canary

Poetry
Science Fiction Saint
Pearl
untitled child

The Western Alienation Merit Badge

a novel

Nancy Jo Cullen

A Buckrider Book

This is a work of fiction. All characters, organizations, places and events portrayed are either products of the author's imagination or are used fictitiously. Any resemblance to actual persons, living or dead; events or locales is entirely coincidental.

© Nancy Jo Cullen, 2019

No part of this publication may be reproduced, stored in a retrieval system or transmitted, in any form or by any means, without the prior written consent of the publisher or a license from the Canadian Copyright Licensing Agency (Access Copyright). For an Access Copyright license, visit www.accesscopyright.ca or call toll free to 1-800-893-5777.

Buckrider Books is an imprint of Wolsak and Wynn Publishers.

Cover and interior design: Michel Vrana
Cover images: assembled from iStockphoto.com
Author photograph: Kristen Ritchie
Typeset in Garamond Premier Pro, Cooper Black, and Futura Std
Printed by Ball Media, Brantford, Canada

10 9 8 7 6 5 4 3 2 1

 Canada Council for the Arts   Conseil des Arts du Canada    ONTARIO ARTS COUNCIL CONSEIL DES ARTS DE L'ONTARIO an Ontario government agency un organisme du gouvernement de l'Ontario    Canadä

The publisher gratefully acknowledges the support of the Canada Council for the Arts, the Ontario Arts Council and the Government of Canada.

Buckrider Books
280 James Street North
Hamilton, ON
Canada L8R 2L3

Library and Archives Canada Cataloguing in Publication

Title: The western alienation merit badge / Nancy Jo Cullen.
Names: Cullen, Nancy Jo, author.
Identifiers: Canadiana 20190061545 | ISBN 9781928088783 (softcover)
Classification: LCC PS8555.U473 W47 2019 | DDC C813/.54—dc23

For Mary Jane, Burke, Debbie, Sue, Mike & Danny,
my sisters and brothers

You will often come across things to do and learn that will relate back to things you have already done and learned.

The Guide Handbook, 1965

After the inland sea dried up and its beaches turned to sandstone and the plant life turned to coal and gas, the ice advanced and ground the stone to dirt, then later retreated from the riparian valleys, coulees and rolling plains where now a girl stepped through the rabbitbush, rough fescue and western wheat grass. She wiped her eyes with the back of her hand, pulled her six-shooter cap gun out of its holster, pointed the pistol in the air and fired. A loud pop and the choking smell of the burning cap, but nothing else. No other creature.

She pulled *The Guide Handbook* from the rear waistband of her cut-offs and turned the blue and white paperback over in her hands. She traced the cloverleaf with the letters GGC on the back cover, mouthed the words *Published by Girl Guides of Canada Guides du Canada 1965* and flipped it open to the foreword. At the bottom of the page she stopped on the sentences: "You are now a Guide Recruit. This book is for you." The girl wiped her eyes again and, sick of crying, she spat on the page. She raised her arm to hurl the book into the field; let the ground squirrels and magpies tear up the pages for their nests. But, after a moment's hesitation, she dropped her arm and tucked the pilfered book back into the waistband of her shorts. Fuck them. She was keeping it because this book was for her, right? Even if she was no goddamn Guide Recruit.

Autumn 1982

Emergency Helper

Frances called home as soon as she got the letter, but Doris had been dead five weeks by the time she reached her dad. She could hear Bernadette in the background, all despair: "Dad, you can't just shake your head. Frankie can't see your face. Use. Words." She sounded ready to blow.

Frances unfolded the letter, sent by her stepmother on July 19. It was written in Doris's perfect script on both sides of a single page.

Dearest Frankie,

I'll be brief. I'm afraid everything has taken a turn for the worse and the doctors haven't given us much hope. I worry about your dad, how he's going to cope after I'm gone. He's very sensitive and he misses you terribly. He's too proud to say so, but I know it to be true.

Bernadette has been a great help driving me to chemo when your dad has had to work, but believe me when I tell you that things have gone from bad to worse. Your dad was laid off. They gave him two weeks and a small package. To be honest, they've done the best they can and let your dad go so Brian, who still has three children living at home, can continue to work. Your dad and I both understand, so many people are losing their jobs, we're lucky he was able to get what he did. He'll have my pension, but it's not much and he'll still have to make mortgage payments. I suppose we should have thought about insurance but we just never did. We just didn't expect something like this so soon.

I know that I'm asking so much of you and I know you just want to be out in the world. And you deserve to be out there being young and free, but I love your father and I think he's going to need you when I'm gone. I wish you would consider coming home. I can't make you return and I wouldn't want to, but I am going to ask you to look into your heart and do what you feel is right.

When you consider what I am asking of you, think also of this: I don't know what the Lord's great plan is, but I believe He has a rationale for everything he puts in front of us. Remember, God doesn't make mistakes. I trust in God's will, and I trust you too, Frankie, to do the right thing.

I am so grateful to have had any time at all with your dad, and with you and Bernie. It's been an absolute pleasure, Frankie, thank you. Don't be afraid to pray for my soul, I'm sure I can use all the help I can get.

With much love and a willing heart,

Doris xo

As if Frances could stay away after that letter, let alone the bloody phone call with her dad all catatonic and Bernie so irate. The letter had taken nearly two months to reach her in Sagres. Working under the table, serving the endless stream of Brits that frolicked on the Portuguese shores had been fun. "For once," she muttered.

"What?" Reena turned her head toward Frankie. She'd been staring listlessly out the window, a cigarette burning between her fingers. Reena refused to stay in Portugal without Frances, refused to let her make the trip back to Gatwick on her own, but had barely spoken to her since she'd made the decision to return to Calgary.

"I'm not angry, Frannie," she'd said. Then she'd kissed Frances and pushed her onto their small bed. "I'd just rather not talk." And so they spent their last night together fucking and drinking sangria. It was a splendid finish to the Algarve, before the long journey by bus, train and ferry back to Gatwick for Frances's flight home. Except now Frances was hungover and ravenous; Reena was chain smoking and punishingly silent, but not angry.

"Nothing," Frances said. "Just talking to myself."

Reena took a drag from her cigarette then crushed it into the ashtray.

"Shit got better when Doris came into the picture," Frances said.

Reena nodded and lit another cigarette.

Doris was into peace and no nukes; she loved Dorothy Day and liberation theology. She even got Frances to read *The Long Loneliness*, hoping, Frances guessed, that it would turn her back into some kind of good Catholic. "But you quit the convent," Frances would argue. "I quit the convent, not God," Doris would say. Then Frances would say, "Well, I quit both." They had that circular argument more than a few times.

Well Doris was dead now and, according to Bernie, their dad was drinking himself into a nightly stupor and crying whenever *Magnum P.I.*, or even an ad for *Magnum P.I.*, came on because it had been their favourite.

"You're going to run out."

Reena shrugged.

The train lurched northward.

On the Channel crossing they sat on the outside deck and Reena started to cry.

"Bugger it," she said.

"I'm sorry," Frances said.

"Well I'm not," Reena snapped.

They parted awkwardly at Victoria Station. Reena wrote down Frances's Calgary address and barely promised to write. They hugged briefly and separated. Because what else could they do? Then Frances was taking off and then the 707 was taxiing toward the Calgary terminal.

Frances glanced out her window, dark construction cranes stood in front of the Calgary Tower, hooks dangling. Red Square her dad and his cronies called it. So she was back, whether she wanted to be or not. Safely landed in Calgary, with its newly bankrupt oil barons, out-of-work rig hands, jobless heavy-duty mechanics and unemployed secretaries. *Yippee yi yo kayah.*

Signaller

 "Nice army boots." Bernie's first words to Frances. "They go with the brush cut."

"Thanks," Frances said sweetly.

Bernie wrapped a single arm around Frances, pulling her close. "Sarcasm, sweetie." She ran her hand across Frances's flattop. "What were you thinking here?"

Frances swung her backpack with her free arm and headed toward the doors.

Bernie fired up a smoke as soon as they got into the car. "I'm trying to quit," she said.

Frances unrolled her window.

"You'll see why it's so hard." Bernie took a long drag on her cigarette.

They drove in silence. Barlow Trail rolled past, the mountains, already dusted with snow, marking the western horizon. Then the Sheraton Hotel, the Husky truck stop, the endless repair and service shops housed in dull beige buildings and, after the impossibly tiny cars of Europe, trucks, all trucks, like the *Jimmy* they were driving, the brand name her dad couldn't resist.

"Poor daddy," Frances said.

Bernadette nodded. "But I have to tell you, he's not so easy to live with right now."

Frances bugged her eyes at Bernadette.

"Sure that shit with Doris was brutal, I mean really, really terrible. But hey, I lost a good job too!" Bernadette tossed her cigarette out the window, the better part of it not smoked. "And the guy I used to work for just died of a massive heart attack. He lost everything. Every fucking thing. You have no idea."

"Give me some credit, Bernie."

Bernadette raised her eyebrows and drove on, eyes on the road, hands tightly gripping the steering wheel, knuckles white.

"Okay, you can roll your window up now," Bernie said.

Frances rolled her window up. The sisters drove in silence toward their father waiting at home.

Jimmy was standing in the window. When Frances stepped out of the truck, he held his hand up – more like a stop signal than a wave. Jesus, he did look crazy. Frances offered a careful wave in return. Jimmy smiled and raised his other hand. He was holding a Pil; he tipped the brightly illustrated green and red label toward her, a salute of sorts, raised the bottle to his mouth and took a long swallow. Then he bent toward the sofa and disappeared from view.

"I know you thought I was exaggerating," Bernie said.

Citizen

Jimmy watched his girls retreat (at last!) into the kitchen. No he didn't want tea, thank you very much. He was trying to watch the news while they nattered on about wherever the hell it was Frankie had been. A guy could hardly hear with that racket. He stood close to the TV and stared down into the set until they got the message. Then he cranked the volume and flopped back into his chair.

Though he had to wonder why he turned the news on day after day. Each report was as bad the last, and sometimes worse. Everybody foaming around the mouth about jobless rates. And now, Jesus H. Murphy, this here election. But maybe Kesler and those separatist kooks would give Lougheed a run for his money. Jimmy swatted at the air. Blah, blah, blah, he wasn't voting anyway.

He didn't give a fuck about any election, or whatever fat cat represented him in Edmonton. Once a guy was in government he did just what he wanted anyway – those jackasses in Ottawa fixing the price of oil against all of Alberta were proof enough of that. Jimmy snorted. Someone was getting rich, but it sure wasn't him. Lord, he wished he could just feel bad about shitty job prospects. It would be a blessing right now to only have to worry about not having a job, and this unnecessary Alberta election, and those bastards in Ottawa. Instead, all he could think about was his dead wife; all he could think about was everything they were never going to have again.

He needed a nap.

He left the TV blaring and went into his room.

Cook

Later, her body clock scrambled, Frances paced the basement, jangly with fatigue. Her dad built her a bedroom and rumpus room right after they moved in, so he and Doris could have privacy. So they could get it on, which she didn't ever like to think about – not then, not now. Jimmy also built himself a workroom that was so disused it was covered in grime. Inside the workroom was a table, and piled against the rear wall was an old tire, a space heater, some Christmas lights and a box of decorations. Frances drew a smiley face in the dust that covered her dad's worktable.

The rumpus room was equipped with her old record player and, next to it, a fourteen-inch black-and-white Toshiba she won in with a raffle ticket purchased from some Rotary Club guy on Stephen Avenue. Now that was a rare bit of good luck. She thumbed through her LPs then placed the Pretenders on the turntable and lay down the length of the navy blue sofa that Jimmy and Doris had scavenged from an alley. A spring pushed into her ass. You get what you pay for – that's what Jimmy would say when she complained about the sofa. On the windowsill sat a maniacal-looking papier-mâché gopher she'd made as a kid. Her stomach churned: meatloaf and the fucking strangeness of absolutely everything here.

Jimmy's dinner plate was piled with meatloaf slathered in ketchup and baked potato smothered in butter and salt. He refused broccoli by spreading both hands, fingers splayed, above his plate.

"No broccoli, Dad?" Bernadette said, all fake chipper.

Jimmy shook his head.

"More for us then!" She tilted the bowl of broccoli over Frances's plate and dropped a heaping mound next to the slice of meatloaf there. The veggies were limp and overcooked.

"Ketchup?" Bernie pushed the bottle toward Frances. "I hope you don't mind, Frankie," she said. "But you're going to see a lot of Dad in the basement. He's going to take up woodworking."

Jimmy raised his head, blinked at Frankie and lifted his beer to his mouth.

"Sounds good," Frances said.

"He's had that room set up for years. It's just going to waste, which is the last thing Doris would have wanted. Doris never believed in waste. Did she, Dad?"

Jimmy kept his head bowed over his plate.

"Well, she didn't," Bernie said. "Doris believed waste was a sin."

Frances nodded.

"Waste is a sin. Don't you agree, Dad?"

Jimmy cut slices of potato and meatloaf and stabbed them with his fork.

Bernie turned her attention to Frances. "You don't like ketchup?"

"Not really," Frances said.

"You used to love ketchup!"

"When I was eleven."

"There's nothing wrong with ketchup."

"I never said there was."

Jimmy speared another piece of potato, another piece of meatloaf.

"There's ketchup in your meatloaf," Bernadette said. "I use Mom's old recipe: ketchup, HP, milk, egg and bread crumbs."

"It's very good," Frances said. "Right, Dad?"

Jimmy nodded in agreement.

"Good luck getting him to talk," Bernie said.

"Thanks for making supper, Bernie."

Bernadette placed her hands on the table, reaching toward Jimmy and Frances as if in supplication. "It is so good to be together again," she said. "I think it will be a healing time for us. It should be a healing time for us."

Frances flipped onto her stomach, the wonky couch spring a punishing comfort. It was nice of her to try, but Bernadette was no Doris. Or it was weird of Bernie to try. Frances was undecided. Doris would definitely have said it was nice of Bernie. She would have said something like, "Chin up, today is the first day of the rest of your life!" You could always count on Doris to say something corny like that.

Frances would have liked to have said goodbye to her.

Be Prepared

Bernadette lay in the dark psychologically preparing for the next day when they were going to put Ken Oliver to rest.

(Down the road, in the late nineties, when she was outselling every other real estate agent in her office, she would shrug her shoulders and tell the other agents she was just lucky. But luck had only the smallest part to do with it; Bernadette had a system. She ran the scenarios in her head time and time again, until she felt prepared for any and every eventuality. Of course, one couldn't be prepared for any and every eventuality, but nine times out of ten Bernadette closed the deal, and she had the Million Dollar Club membership to prove it.)

Because times were so hard, tomorrow when she smiled she had to make certain it reached her eyes. She had to keep eye contact and she had to shake hands firmly. She calmed herself by rubbing the hard, round scar on her left palm and ran through the list of men, former co-workers, that she expected to see.

Butch Keller hit the bottle hard after he lost his job and his wife finally left him, so Bernadette wouldn't ask after her. Ted Hardy had a new grandson – a little bit of something even guys down on their luck could celebrate. She would save a hug for Raymond and Glen, who had spent so many hours on the road servicing the rigs. Neither one of them had been able to find work yet and Raymond actually cried the last time she'd seen him. He'd come into the bar to say hi, and she poured him a rye and coke and told him it was on the house. That set off the water works. She wouldn't bring that up either.

There was going to be a reception in the church hall after the funeral, which seemed the ultimate insult to Ken Oliver, high-flying oilman that he was. Sandwiches and coffee, his ex must really hate him. But Bernadette would be extremely polite to Gloria Oliver because Ken would expect no less of her.

And then afterward Bernadette would see if some of the guys wanted to go for a drink, to raise a toast to Ken Oliver, reduced to nothing but the shirt on his back by declining energy values, fucking made-in-Canada oil pricing and a little unfortunate planning. Because Bernadette was still Ken Oliver's secretary, whether anybody knew it or not.

Needleworker

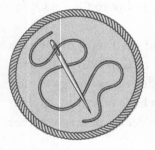The house was silent and gloomy in the half-light of dawn. Jimmy switched on a lamp and opened his book, *Crochet for Beginners: From Simple Squares to Afghan Blankets*. Page six. It had turned his crank to watch Doris while she crocheted. There was a rhythm to her left hand (the raised index finger, the closed middle finger and thumb) that called to mind other things: her hand moving down his torso, and farther still. Even now it heated him up to think of her industrious fingers. But Jimmy shook off that line of thought; he made a slipknot with his practice yarn and dropped it over the crochet hook. After that, things got tricky.

The first chain, now that was pretty straightforward. It was just under and over and pull it through until he had linked twenty-one stitches. How in hell he was supposed to hold the damn yarn between his middle finger and thumb while supporting the yarn on his index finger – Christ, what did that even mean? – was the mystery. His grip was so tense that his stitches came out too tight to insert the crochet hook for the next row. Jimmy closed his eyes, pushed his thumb into the bridge of his nose.

Not even the shit in this life that looked easy was easy. Bernadette thought he could make himself happy building birdhouses, and he supposed she meant well, but her constant harping was going to send him over the bloody edge. As if it had been his plan to bust his ass his entire life so he could end up out of work at fifty-three with another dead wife, and nearly homeless too, if it weren't for the kids pitching in. A humiliation those girls couldn't fathom.

The only fight he'd ever had with Doris had come on the heels of her saying that maybe it was a good idea to have a national plan for oil, to take care of our own first, and Jimmy had bugged out his eyes and sputtered, "Who the fuck is taking care of us?"

Doris turned away from him then. "I'm not saying it's perfect," she said, "but either we're a country together or a country divided."

"Oh, we're a country divided," he answered, "and you have your Frog boyfriend to thank for that."

Doris had just begun chemo and there he was going apeshit. What kind of an asshole was he? He apologized, and Doris held him close and said, "I don't know why things are so hard, Jimmy, but I expect we'll understand one day." Jimmy didn't say, yeah, when hell freezes over, but he thought it, and Doris slapped his arm and said, "You've got to have hope, Jimmy!"

"I do, baby," he told her, but already her pretty brown hair was coming out in chunks.

Jimmy tugged out his stitches and slipped a fresh loop over the crochet hook. He looked carefully at the diagram again, wrapped the yarn around the hook and pulled it slowly through the loop. Never, in all his days, would he have imagined himself sitting in his chair hunched over a crochet needle for all he was worth. He could pretty much hear what the guys at work would have said if they'd seen him. They'd have given him a nickname – Grandma, or some such thing. Well, there was no chance of that now, and what a man did in the privacy of his own home was between him and God.

"Hey, Dad, what are you doing there?" Bernadette walked into the living room, tightening a robe around her waist.

Correction: what a man did in the privacy of his own home was between him, God and his daughters. Jimmy held up the thin line of his work for Bernadette to see.

"Crochet?" she squeaked. "Really?"

Bernadette just stood there watching him. Well bully for her.

She sighed. "Why don't we get you set up in the basement? You could make a birdhouse or something."

Jimmy kept his head down.

"I'm going to make a coffee. Would you like one?"

He shook his head.

"Suit yourself," she said. She marched to the curtains and yanked them open, "How about a little daylight, at least?"

After Bernie left, all decked out in her funeral attire, Jimmy made himself a bologna sandwich and a cup of coffee. Frances, wrapped in a blanket, wandered into the living room during *The Price is Right* and flopped down on the couch. By then Jimmy had pulled out his stitches again and begun a third time on his first granny square, and it was already looking a damn sight better than his earlier efforts.

"What do you got going there?" she asked.

Jimmy held up his growing square.

Frances laughed, "Way to keep it weird, Dad."

Jimmy just smiled. Today he was going to be easy come, easy go.

Frances hunkered down in her blanket and in no time at all was back asleep. Jimmy would be lying if he said it wasn't good to see her again, but she was snoring on his couch, making it hard to hear Bob Barker.

Good Turn

"Frankie, hey!" Bernadette knocked on Frances's cheek several times in quick succession.

Frances pushed Bernie's hand off and opened her eyes.

"Look who's here." Bernie stepped out of the way. A young woman, dressed in all black – thrift store cowboy boots, fishnet stockings and a vintage fifties dress – raised her right hand to her shoulder and offered a three-finger salute. Instead of natural blonde, her hair was dyed fire engine red, backcombed and teased into a frantic halo. There were signs of makeup: partially wiped black smudges under her eyes and a red stain on her lips. Frances recognized her immediately.

"I don't know how I didn't put it together all these years," Bernadette said to Frances. "If I'd known her dad was my boss. What a scream that would have been." She looked at the young woman – Robyn. "Your dad would have got such a kick out of that."

Frances blinked and acted dumb.

Bernie clapped her hands together.

"Robyn Oliver," said Robyn.

"Oh, hi," Frances said.

"Long time no see."

"Getting close to ten years," Bernie said. "I know that for sure."

"You haven't changed a bit," Robyn said. "I would have known you if I walked past you on the street."

"She's jet lagged," Bernie said as an explanation for Frances's silence. Then to Frances, "I've invited Robyn to stay here. She'll take the couch in the rec room. I didn't think you'd mind."

So typical of Bernie to offer a space that wasn't hers. "No, I don't mind."

"Sit up." Bernie smacked Frances's legs.

"Small world," Robyn said.

Frances sat up. "Sorry about your dad."

Robyn shrugged, "I can't say it was a surprise."

"Bernie said it was rough."

"They lost their house. My mom got fed up."

"The one on the lake?"

Robyn nodded, "He used it to underwrite the company. So Mom went back to Toronto. I stayed here. I just broke up with my boyfriend. Well, Graham wasn't really my boyfriend. He thought he was my boyfriend."

Frances nodded.

"He's not very happy with me right now. I can't take his attitude." She sighed, "I've got to go get my stuff."

"We'll take you," Bernie said. "He won't give you any attitude with us around."

"I've already got plans," Frances said.

"Cancel them! We're on a mission."

"I made plans to go see an old friend," Frances lied. "Joanne."

"We can go tomorrow."

"Just go without me." Frances stood up. "I've got to get ready."

Robyn hugged her. "It's great to see you again, Frankie."

"You too," Frances said.

In the basement Frances pulled on a clean white T-shirt, laced up her boots, grabbed her leather jacket and split before she could be cornered and offered a ride downtown.

Neighbourhood

 It was hot and her jacket felt like fifty pounds; its collar scratched at the back of her neck. Whatever – it suited her mood after Bernie showed up with Robyn fucking Oliver in tow. Bernie had the intuition of a rock and, evidently, the memory of a gnat. Why else would she bring Robyn back around?

Frances shrugged her jacket off and tied it around her hips. A squealing Honda Civic pulled out of the McDonald's lot. She counted six teenaged boys crammed into the vehicle, the two sharing the front passenger seat loudly denying their homosexual attraction. Kids like that were exactly the reason why she had no friends in high school.

Her eyes lit upon a handwritten sign taped to the door of a restaurant on the east end of a short strip of shops that included Big Convenience, Dover Used Appliances, a locked glass door that led to a second floor of offices and Bar None Pizza & Steak House. The sign, scrawled in ballpoint pen, read: "Help Wanted: Dishwasher."

The restaurant was darkly lit and furnished with heavy wood tables and chairs. A tired-looking woman sat at the bar, smoking a cigarette and flipping through the paper. She nodded at Frances and tucked a piece of her black hair behind her ear. "Hello." She had the voice of someone who'd spent ten years yelling.

"I'm here about the job."

"You have to lift thirty pounds." She sighed heavily and pushed herself up from the barstool. "Wait here."

She returned with a fat, balding man wearing a white T-shirt, black chef pants and clogs. "You have to lift thirty pounds," he said.

"I can lift thirty pounds," Frances said.

"You have to work Thursday to Sunday. Nights. Four bucks an hour. Plus tips."

"Sure."

He checked his watch. "Come back tomorrow," he said. "At four. Don't be late." He walked back into the kitchen.

"What's your name, sweetheart?" the woman asked.

"Frances."

"I'm Rita. That's Tomas. He doesn't mean to be a prick. Our dishwasher is my brother-in-law, but he's, you know, simple. Too much stress and he loses it. And Tomas, he's all worked up right now, busy or no customers. And then Oscar is crying." She took a deep breath. "Just so you know."

"Sure," Frances said.

"We'll see you tomorrow then." Rita climbed back on the stool, took a final drag on her cigarette and pressed it into the glass ashtray.

"See you," Frances said, and turned to leave. Outside, after the dark of the restaurant, the sun burned her eyes.

Rescuer

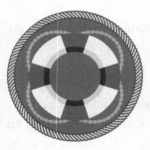

Frances slipped into the basement as soon as she returned from her mercifully brief job search. So what if the place was sketchy? She lay on the couch and drifted into a murky, jet-lagged sleep, then woke to the sound of a truck stopping in front of the house, its radio blasting "Echo Beach, far away in time" – then the song went silent as the engine was cut, followed by the slamming of a door. She crept to the window and watched Bernie wander up the lawn. No Robyn. Bernadette spotted Frances, waved then drew her finger across her neck as though she were slicing it with a knife. She crouched at the window.

Frances slid the glass open. "Where's Robyn?"

"She stomped off in a huff."

"You're totally wasted."

"A little," Bernadette said.

"What happened to Robyn?"

"Did you know that idiot likes Trudeau? After everything that happened to her dad."

"Where did she go?"

Bernadette shrugged.

"Where did you leave her?"

"Correction: she left me."

"How much have you had to drink?"

"She left me with half a jug."

"Where were you guys?"

"I've had about a jug, plus a little bit."

"I thought you were helping her."

"She's a big girl."

"I thought you looooved her."

"I looooved her dad."

"You gave her my couch."

"But not in the biblical sense," Bernadette said. "He was always very professional."

"Are you not at all worried about Robyn?"

"I'm worried about anyone that would vote Liberal, including you."

"What makes you think I'd vote Liberal?"

"You wouldn't?" Bernadette clutched her chest. "Thank Christ."

Frances laughed at her sister's dramatic misunderstanding. So what if Bernie thought she would vote Conservative – which Frances would never do, even if you paid her.

Bernadette took a deep breath. "Frankie?"

"Yes?"

"Can you open the goddamn front door?"

"Does Robyn have any money?"

"I doubt it."

Frances shut the window and headed up to let Bernadette in. At the door she put out her hand. "Give me the keys."

Bernadette dropped them into her palm. "I should have worn a sweater."

"Where was she staying?"

"On Thirteenth. Close to Tenth. Southwest."

Frances strode to the truck.

"Bring home chips," Bernadette called after her.

Robyn was easy enough to find. She was sitting on her duffle bag in front of a white, three-storey walk-up, a six-pack at her feet. She held a smoke in her left hand and a bottle of Blue in her right. Frances parked the truck and got out.

"You can stay with us."

"Your sister is a trip."

"Don't worry about Bernie. She's just a lot of hot air."

"I got the impression you weren't too happy to see me."

"I was just surprised."

"I locked my key inside Graham's place."

"Well, you can't stay here."

Robyn shrugged. "It wouldn't kill me. I can totally make Graham take me back. He loves me." Robyn flicked her cigarette onto the street.

Frances opened the passenger door. "Get in."

"If you're really okay with it."

"I'm really okay with it."

Robyn saluted, "Yessir."

A ripple of delight tracked across Frances's belly. There was no denying that Robyn was cute as ever.

Conservationist

 Jimmy was well aware that a couple of girls were sleeping in his basement, but he'd done everything he could upstairs and needed to get into his workroom. He had packed a box with yarn that Doris managed to stash in their closet and, on the upper shelf, he'd found two more boxes filled with assorted fabric. He'd hauled her portable sewing machine out of the linen closet, as well as the ironing board and iron. He'd sat at the kitchen table and had another cup of coffee and a smoke and still not a sound from below. Must be nice to be able to sleep your days away.

The idea of the Kenmore woke him like a shot in the middle of the night. The sewing machine! Jimmy was certain it could be the ticket to preserving his life with Doris, to keeping up with her, wherever she was. He had even been threading the thing for her after her chemo fingers became too stiff to fuss with the spool and bobbin. A machine, a pedal – those were the kinds of things that made sense to Jimmy. He'd been up since four thirty getting ready, energized with the idea that if he just set himself up right he and Doris could carry on a conversation for all eternity or until he croaked, whichever came first, *ha ha*. And with that in mind, and sick to death of waiting, he stacked the three boxes and carried them on down.

He could tell the girl on the couch, Ken Oliver's kid, was faking sleep. She was watching him from under her lashes as he brought the boxes into his workroom. What a goddamn mess that place was. Some smartass had drawn a smiley face in the middle of the grimy tabletop. Jimmy pulled out the broom tucked behind the water heater and pushed the dust from the table. An army of particles rose and advanced toward Jimmy. He sneezed twice.

"Hey, Dad." Frances was standing in the doorway. "What are you up to?"

Her severe hair! And she was such a pretty girl. Maybe she was thinking of taking holy orders. Stranger things had happened.

"Dad?"

"Organizing my workroom, like your sister said."

"With fabric and yarn?"

"Yup."

"Whatever floats your boat."

"That's right."

"When I was little my mom hired a house painter who knit his own socks," the kid on the couch said.

Jimmy smiled then headed back up to the kitchen to fill a bucket with soap and water.

"You don't think it's weird?" Frances asked.

"Weird's okay," Robyn said. She grabbed a smoke from her bag and knocked over an empty mickey of vodka. It clattered against the concrete. Robyn grimaced. "Man, I've got a headache."

Frances stepped into the workroom and grabbed the space heater off the utility shelf. It would come in handy sooner or later. Autumn in Calgary was short. After Labour Day you might get a little summer and, after the equinox, even a little more. But snow and cold could happen any time after Thanksgiving. She was going to be prepared.

Jimmy returned and set his bucket of soapy water on the floor. Water rose with the motion and slopped over the sides. He pulled a dripping sponge out of the bucket and ran it across the table.

Frances held up the heater. "You mind if I take this?"

Jimmy shook his head. "Nope." He turned his attention back to his work and began humming "Make the World Go Away," which had been with him for weeks now. The girls weren't taking the hint so Jimmy started to sing to himself as he scrubbed. He tried not to let the force of Doris's absence push up his throat. He clenched his teeth against all the surprise and misery that tightened the air in the room. He held onto the worktable and ferociously pushed the sponge across the wood surface. Then the crying started. At first, Jimmy quietly wiped his cheeks on his shoulders, but the tears took on a force of their own and he gave into the sorrow, sucking in air in short gasps, his face a mess of snot and dust and tears. When there was nothing to do but weep, God help him, a guy wept.

He lifted his head to order the girls to just leave but they had already made a soundless exit.

Frances sat at the table. Robyn leaned against the kitchen counter and lit a half joint she pulled out of her bag. "Shit," she said.

She passed the joint to Frances, but Frances shook her head. "Things are weird enough."

"Hmmm," Robyn said.

Robyn was a million miles from the Robyn that Frances remembered.

"You're exactly like I remember you," Robyn said.

"You too," Frances said.

Robyn pointed her finger at Frances and shook it. "We're going to have so much fun hanging out.

Frances smiled.

Creative Drama

Bernadette lit a smoke as soon as the two cops from the fraud division left. They came in to ask her a few questions about Robert Martel, aka Mitch Miller, aka Austin Stevens – which she couldn't believe anyone fell for, although, to be fair, she never gave the name Mitch Miller a second thought. And even though it could get her fired she poured a big slug of rum into her coffee, because she just needed to calm the fuck down.

Right as Doris hit her last couple of weeks of life, Bobby Dees acquired a new regular, a hunky suit with a movie star name: Mitch Miller. He came in for lunch near the end of the rush and sat at her bar. He drank gin martinis, dry with olives and a twist. The first time she took his order he said, "If I were your boss, I'd have given you the Veronica name tag."

"Only Bettys and Peggy-Sues here," she said.

From there things progressed to the usual question, "How come a pretty girl like you isn't married?"

"How do you know I'm not?"

"No ring."

"You're assuming I want to be married."

"Not at all. Because if you were, I'm sure you'd be wearing a ring." Mitch pushed a five-dollar bill across the bar. "Why don't you put some Baileys in your coffee?"

"Don't mind if I do." Bernadette rang in the drink and poured a healthy shot of Baileys into her coffee.

On another visit he said, "How about you give me your number?"

She shook her head. "No."

"You don't like me?"

"I don't know you." She focused her attention back on her work, a bus tray full of dirty glasses waiting to be loaded into the dishwasher. She didn't have the energy to be flirting with customers. She barely had the energy to be at work, but they'd still have to pay the mortgage after Doris died.

She gave the guy points for persistence. Each time he showed up for lunch he asked for her number. Each time he asked, she refused. Anyway, even if she was interested in giving him her number, good God, what if her dad answered the phone? It was too much to explain what was going on.

August 18, two weeks to the day after Doris died, Mitch came in just as she was leaving.

"You're done?"

"I'm back at five. Split shift."

"Well then, maybe I should take you out for a drink."

"I didn't bring a change of clothes."

He shrugged. "I think you look great."

"Isn't your boss going to wonder where you are?"

"I'm my own boss."

"Lucky you."

They sat in a corner. He ordered his usual, she ordered a Bloody Mary. He smelled faintly of Old Spice. He was new to Calgary. He'd come on the heels of the National Energy Program in early '81, but had managed to earn a living by helping guys who'd lost their jobs manage their debt. Mitch kept his eyes on hers while they talked. He told her about homeowners so overwhelmed by unmanageable mortgages they practically begged him to buy their houses. Mitch had a small inheritance to spend so it was a win-win – he took over the houses and they stayed on as tenants.

She loosened up with the drink, not to mention his frank eye contact.

"Perhaps you'd like to see this space I'm thinking of renting." Mitch held up a single key on a blue plastic fob. "It's up Barlow Trail, but I'd have a great view of the mountains."

"Now?"

"I'm interested in your opinion. It's your hometown, you know it better than me."

Bernadette shrugged. "Why not?"

Mitch drove a blue '76 Stingray. He opened the door for her; she lowered herself into the car and unlocked his side. He climbed into the driver's seat, leaned across and kissed her. And, to give credit where credit is due, he made a fine job of it. The kiss was followed by a jolt of loosening between her legs, between her shoulders and in her brain, then the decision to fuck him, to just let her body lead for once. Mitch turned the key in the ignition and the engine growled to life. Fitting. Bernadette crossed her legs and her dress slipped up toward her thighs. She didn't pull the hem back down, but looked straight ahead, nonchalant, like she was the hot star in some hot movie. Because didn't she deserve a little fun?

The view of the mountains stretching across the horizon, newly capped with snow, was never going to get old. Otherwise, Mitch's prospective office space was as ordinary as any other: dull brown carpet, beige walls, fluorescent ceiling lights, including one in the reception area with a cracked cover. The whole place smelled of dust that had settled deep into the flooring. An armless, metal-trimmed chair, upholstered in black vinyl, was the only piece of furniture in the entire space.

Mitch sat on the chair, his underwear and pants pooled around his ankles. Bernadette straddled him, her dress hiked above her waist. The whole thing was over in less time than it took to hard boil an egg. Bernadette always thought fucking should take longer, but at roughly four minutes into their encounter she cried, "Oh Jesus!" and dug her fingers into Mitch's shoulders, climaxing with her usual fusion of shame for coming so fast and relief for coming before he did. A minute later Mitch pulled her down firmly, shuddered and groaned through his teeth. They remained in the chair, breathing heavily. Bernadette pushed herself off Mitch when she felt warm semen leaking onto the top of her thigh. Her pantyhose were ruined. She rolled them into a ball and stuffed them into her purse. Slipped her feet back into her shoes.

Mitch zipped and buttoned his pants then looked at his watch. "I have a four o'clock meeting with the bank," he said. "Then I'm up to Edmonton for the weekend."

"Sounds busy." She grabbed his suit jacket from the floor and passed it to him.

Mitch pulled her into his arms and kissed her. "You're gorgeous."

Bernadette sneezed into his chest. "So much dust," she said.

Mitch had been blowing smoke up everyone's ass. Those suckers thought they'd solved their money problems when he took their rent, but not a penny of it had been put on their mortgages for the past year. Now the bank was foreclosing on their homes and decent guys were struggling to find a place to live. They were down, then they were kicked by Mitch, or whoever the fuck he was. Of course Mitch had split with the cash. So, it was a relief to honestly tell the cops that she hardly knew the guy, that once she'd gone for a spin in his corvette and had a couple of drinks with him between shifts.

There wasn't a hope in hell she was ever going to tell them she fucked the man.

Sport

Happy hour at Tom's: four tables; average age of customer, impossible to say, but definitely no less than decrepit; beer gut city and one lady hacking up a lung at the bar. Frances was waiting for Tomas to finish something in the back alley, an under-the-table meat deal or some other business he wanted no witness to. She popped a French fry dripping with gravy into her mouth then pushed the plate of fries closer to Tomas's brother, Oscar.

He was long and bony, his hair shaved close to his head. Rita told Frances that the cord had been wrapped tight around Oscar's neck when he was born and that's why he was simple. That's why he was her responsibility, hers and Tomas's, because they were all Oscar had in the world – whatever family Tomas and Oscar once had were dead or lost to migration.

Oscar, to quote him, was "pleased as punch" to meet her. Frances was happy to meet Oscar, too, who balanced Tomas's curt presence with his enthusiasm. He'd talked non-stop until Tomas shouted,

"Shut the fuck up, would you?" And Oscar stopped immediately, untied his apron and walked out of the kitchen. "Jesus Christ," Tomas muttered under his breath. Then Rita marched into the kitchen, pointed a silent finger at her husband and turned on her heels and marched back out.

Now Oscar was drinking Coke and reading *Mad* magazine, happy again and chatty.

Tomas walked into the bar. He put his hand on Oscar's shoulder and squeezed. "Sorry, pal."

Oscar patted Tomas's hand. "Sorry, pal," he said.

"Come on, sport, back at it," Tomas said to Frances.

It wasn't so bad as far as jobs went; Frances had had worse. And she'd rather work the dish pit where at least she didn't have to talk to customers she couldn't stand. Frances enjoyed Oscar's chatter, but then again she didn't have to live with him twenty-four seven. Tom's had a small rush at happy hour, which, for her, mostly involved trying to scrub the burnt cheese from a few nacho platters. Most nights the short-lived rush tapered off to pretty much nothing, just a table of pensioners drinking through their retirement.

And even though he wasn't non-stop like Oscar, Tomas liked to talk, too. He came at Frances with a series of invasive questions.

"You got a boyfriend?" he asked.

"No," Frances said.

Tomas looked at her like he was trying to probe her mind. Frances stared back.

Tomas nodded. "Your dad's out of work?" he said. "Since when?"

When she told him about Doris dying and her dad getting laid off, Tomas just shook his head.

"Your sister got a husband?" he asked.

"No," she said.

"What's the matter with you girls?" He vigorously chopped an onion into tiny pieces. "I'm not even going to ask about you because

I don't believe in asking about things you don't want to know, but how old is your sister?"

"Twenty-five."

"Is she even looking for a husband?"

"How would I know?"

"Don't sisters tell each other everything?"

"Apparently not," Frances said.

In an effort to get Tomas onto a different subject, and because she'd washed every dish in the place, Frances asked if he'd maybe show her how to use the knife like that. She'd like to be able to chop an onion like a real cook. Tomas puffed up his chest and pulled a knife out of a drawer and said, "Learn from a master," then winked at her.

So yeah, it could have been worse. She could have had no job, instead of a job in a mostly dead restaurant with not the worst people in the world. Once, Tomas had had ambitions to serve the entire oil field on their way in and out of town, and catering, too. Now he was just trying not to default on his lease.

"Yada yada yada," Rita said.

Junior Camper

 As soon as she realized she'd missed her period Bernadette puked. It was the excitement, even if morning sickness was about to take her down. Although in her case, it could hardly be referred to as "morning" sickness. The urge to vomit struck Bernadette at any hour.

(A decade later, after a good number of *Donahue* and *Oprah* episodes, when it finally sunk in that AIDS wasn't something that just killed gay men, Bernadette was overcome again with nausea – anxiety this time. She spent the following six months riddled with remorse and fear that the virus lay dormant in her, just waiting for its moment to smite her and leave Brandon orphaned in the care of her doddering father, who was fine and dandy for babysitting but, even if he wanted to, completely unfit for the task of raising a nine-year-old boy.

And although she'd been celibate for years, repentant even, and was working on transmuting her sexual energy into a worthy outlet, more than once she'd been led by her craven desires. Why shouldn't she be punished, too? And really, why shouldn't the boom fall just as she was achieving a modicum of financial success?)

But when she first realized that she was ninety-nine percent likely to be pregnant – that there was a tiny being setting up camp inside her body – oh the joy! Everybody would love a baby. Her dad would love a baby. Frankie would love a baby. They needed a baby. They *deserved* a baby. They truly deserved something nice. Except for Mitch. He deserved to rot in hell.

She saw Mitch just once after their so-called date. He seated himself at the bar while she was busy at a table, and when she returned and found him sitting there, all cocky and certain she was dying to fuck him again, she was lit by a flare of rage – partly because she would have liked to have a go at him again and partly because he was wearing too much cologne and believed that a wink and a cocktail was enough to get her back in the sack. So she blew him off. She turned on the chill and finally Mitch said, "I can take a hint," slapped a ten-dollar bill on the bar and left. It stung her a little to see him walk out of the bar. She thought he might have fought harder for her, that their little date had been worth more than ten bucks to him.

It was just her luck that the one person she'd screwed in the better part of the past year was a scam artist of the first order. And it was more of that same luck that she would get knocked up by a lying shit. It wasn't going to give her one second of regret to tell everyone that he was dead. He might just as well be – what kid would want to know they had a dad like Mitch? A lie told for the greater good was pretty much the same thing as telling the truth.

And even though it wasn't much of a problem to be an unwed mother these days, it wasn't all happy anticipation for Bernadette, because the Murrays had a new problem now. Her dad was spending hours in his workroom, sewing. Apparently, he couldn't just stick to knitting. He'd set up a floor lamp, an ironing board and a transistor radio. He sawed down the legs of his worktable so he could manage the sewing machine pedal and placed Doris's Kenmore in the middle of the room so anyone could see what was going on, except for the fact that he kept the door locked tight and she and Frankie were barred from entering. He was working on a project, he said, and when he was ready, he would let them in. What kind of a fifty-three-year-old man took up sewing? She'd seen people resort to some pretty extreme measures this past year, but still. Grief couldn't be an excuse for everything. She worried her dad was having a total breakdown. Hopefully a grandchild would help him focus on important things.

Home Defence

Because Rita was set up in the kitchen reconciling the books, Frances was working the floor, which consisted of three tight-fisted regulars who tipped so poorly it was an insult. She got that they were broke, but if they were too broke to tip, you'd think they'd be smart enough to drink at home. That way they could clean up after themselves and she wouldn't have to listen to their endless bitching. They wouldn't shut up about a toilet repair that they had been forced to pay for because their landlord was nowhere to be found. (And still they had the money to come to the bar and not tip!) Their friend shouted, "Just take it off the fucking rent."

Oscar said, "Uh oh."

And Robyn, who was standing at the bar next to a new, interchangeable boyfriend (another black jeans, black T-shirt, black-leather jacket boy who was opposed to friendliness), leaned toward Oscar and said, "Don't you hate it when people fucking swear?"

Oscar blushed.

"Cut it out," Frances said. She filled up a pint glass with Coke and ice and pushed it across the bar to Oscar.

"Thank you, Frances."

"At home we call her Frankie," Robyn said.

"That's a boy's name," Oscar said.

"It's a nickname, Oscar."

The drunks cackled loudly. Their ashtray was overflowing but Frances couldn't bring herself to care.

"Frances is a pretty name," Oscar said. "Like you."

The newest boyfriend snorted into his beer.

Robyn, eyes on Frances, pushed herself back into her boyfriend and pulled his arms around her. "Frances *is* beautiful," she said. Her boyfriend bristled.

Frances grabbed a clean ashtray and went to collect the dirty one. When she returned the boyfriend was laughing.

"I don't get it," Oscar said.

"Get what?" Frances asked.

"I just told them about Jimmy. You know, the sewing room?"

"So what?" Frances emptied the ashtray into the garbage and tossed it into the bus bin where it clattered loudly against the small pile of dishes.

Robyn lit a smoke. "I think it's cool." She tilted her head and exhaled toward the ceiling.

"I wouldn't be surprised if your old man's a faggot," the boy-friend said.

"Said the guy who wants to do me up the ass," Robyn said.

Oscar gasped.

Frances pointed to the door. "You two need to leave."

"He's leaving right now," Robyn said, pushing the boyfriend away.

"It was a joke!" the boyfriend said.

"Do you see anyone laughing?" Robyn scowled at him.

"You need to relax."

"You need to fuck off."

Oscar gasped.

Frances marched to the door and opened it. "Either one, or both of you, get out. Now."

Robyn walked to the other side of Oscar and sat on a bar stool, refusing to look at her date.

The boyfriend grabbed his cigarettes and jumped off his stool. "I hope I never see you dykes again."

Frances let the door close behind the jackass.

"He was mean," Oscar said.

"I suppose my dad is a little weird."

Robyn shook her head. "Anyway, I'm not a dyke."

Frances nodded.

"Rita sews, too. She makes my pyjama pants," Oscar said.

Sewing

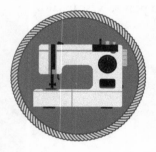

Well of course he knew it looked odd, an old fart like him taking up sewing, but much to his surprise, sewing made sense to Jimmy. He liked the words of the sewing machine: tension and timing, thread and bobbin, presser foot. It felt as natural to him as driving, which he always knew he was born to do. It was a powerful, good feeling to have a foot control under his shoe like a gas pedal, the surge of the needle and fabric as he took off on a seam that was its own particular highway. And because sewing involved mechanics, he felt confident around the machine. So what if the kids didn't like it? Jesus Murphy, he could write a long list of things he didn't like to see his kids doing.

It wasn't easy, learning the pressure of the foot control; not going so fast that he was flying off, hell bent on some seam with stitches all willy-nilly and not strong enough to hold. He quickly learned that slow and steady kept a straight seam and strong stitches. Light pressure from the foot applied just so to the pedal control, his hands guiding (not pulling!) the fabric under the pressure of his foot and through the machine. He had a lot of puckered little pieces sitting in a trashcan to show for that lesson.

He'd found a book, *The Time-Honored Art of Patchwork Quilt Making*, at the library. It made more sense than trying to sew a skirt, and he was surely not capable of making himself a cowboy shirt like the one Doris had made him for the Stampede. He knew enough to start small, with a traditional patchwork square pattern, hourglass shaped, in celebration of his wife. He'd cut up ten five-inch squares in various printed fabrics Doris had used in skirts and blouses and aprons, and then cut up ten more squares in navy blue. The iron was plugged in and set to high, and Jimmy was about to construct his first patchwork square. He'd laid his old hammer across the pages of the book, holding open the step-by-step instructions. If it didn't work, he'd chuck the square out and begin again, no big deal. Jimmy was as ready as he'd ever be.

He lit a smoke and ran his hand across the top of the machine, touching where Doris had touched, feeling what Doris had felt. He set his cigarette in the ashtray, grabbed his first two pieces of fabric and pulled his chair closer to the table, gently kicking the foot control into position. Jimmy dropped the presser foot down, turned the handwheel slowly, manually creating the first stitches, then depressed the reverse control with his right hand and carefully applied pressure to the sewing pedal. The needle moved backward; Jimmy released the reverse control and the stitches moved forward again until he'd finished his first seam. He clipped the threads and removed the square, popped his smoke between his teeth and moved to the ironing board. He pressed the seam flat and held the fabric up to the light. Not half bad.

"Well, hey there," he said. Then he pulled the cigarette from his mouth and stabbed it out in the ashtray. He only had a couple of hours before Bernadette got home from work and started asking questions. He was going to have to motor through his work if he didn't want to be subject to another interrogation tonight.

Bird Lover

On the walk home from Tom's, Robyn said, "Seriously, Frankie, you are beautiful." She took Frances's hand and kissed her palm.

Frances yanked her hand away. "Jesus, Robyn. Where the fuck is that coming from?"

"What? I can't find you attractive?"

"No." Frances blushed. "I mean yes. But it's totally out of the blue."

"Not really."

"Actually, really."

"I've always liked you."

Frances shrugged. "You *like* a lot of people, Robyn."

Robyn pulled Frances close. "But I particularly like you."

Frances pushed her away. "Are you trying to get us beat up?"

"Who's going to beat up two girls?"

"What planet are you living on?"

"Look around." Robyn pointed to the buildings that lined the sidewalk. "No lights. Everyone is home asleep, killjoy." She walked away, pulled a joint out of her cigarette pack and lit up.

Frances kept pace with Robyn, who didn't pass the joint to her – not that Frances would have taken it. "Anyway, I thought you weren't a dyke."

Robyn shrugged. "I'm not."

"So you're just screwing with me?"

"When did you stop knowing how to have fun?"

"I know how to have fun."

Robyn snorted, pinched the end of her joint and tucked it back into her cigarette pack.

They walked without talking, Robyn's boots clicking loudly against the sidewalk. The mood soured.

"Shortcut!" Robyn took an abrupt right onto a side street.

Frances followed Robyn down the sidewalk and into an alley. Robyn turned and shoved her against a garage door. She pushed her full weight against Frances and kissed her, pressing her tongue into Frances's mouth, running her hand up Frances's shirt. Frances sighed and let her body open.

"Maybe you do know how to have fun after all," Robyn said.

Frances took Robyn's wrists, deftly reversed their positions and pinned her against the garage. She reached her hand under Robyn's skirt, pulled down her tights and pushed her fingers up into Robyn.

"Trust me," Frances pulled at Robyn's bottom lip with her teeth, "I know how to have fun."

Robyn sucked in her breath and pulled Frances closer. "You're starting to convince me."

Bernadette was at the table when they walked in. She raised her eyebrows in their direction and lifted a mug to her lips. A flash of panic tore through Frances's chest. It seemed impossible that

Bernie wouldn't notice the charge between her and Robyn, the space between their bodies humming.

"Busy?" Bernadette asked Frances. She hadn't spoken to Robyn since their short night in the pub.

"Totally dead."

"Same here," Bernie said.

Robyn brushed past Frances, her fingers trailing across Frances's thighs. She pulled out a chair and sat down next to Bernadette. Robyn breathed deeply. "Mmmm, peppermint."

"Time to turn in," Bernadette said. She stood up. "Keep it down. Dad just went to bed after spending hours –" she pointed to the basement. "You know. And don't leave the kitchen in a mess."

"Sure thing, Mom," Frances said.

"I'm just saying I don't want to be cleaning up after you."

"You're the one leaving your cup."

Bernadette snatched her cup. Tea splattered across the table. "I mean it, Frankie. I have better things to do than to tidy up after you."

"When is the last time you tidied up after me?"

Bernadette glared at her sister.

"Nineteen seventy-four by my calculation," Frances said.

Bernie marched out of the room.

Frances wiped the table.

"Is she getting her period or something?" Robyn said.

Frances shrugged. "Welcome to my world."

Robyn pulled Frances onto her lap and tugged her T-shirt out from her jeans. "I like your world."

Frances stood up. "Not here." She took Robyn's hand. "Let's go downstairs."

First Aid

Bernadette knelt on the floor beside her bed and rested her head on the mattress. She had no plans of alerting anyone to her situation by barfing. God almighty, she hated this part of being pregnant. She inhaled deeply through her nose, ground her teeth together. Frankie was so full of herself now. And her stupid friend – she must have driven Ken nuts. Poor Ken, his bad-luck end of life punctuated by a bitch wife and a slut daughter.

Bile surged up her throat – Bernie pressed her lips tightly, tried breathing rapidly in and out through her nose. She tried to distract herself, thinking about a sweet little baby and his (or her!) impossibly small fingernails, impossibly soft hair.

And anyway, why did Frances even want to hang around with Robyn? Surely she had better friends than Robyn in this city – she'd only graduated a couple of years ago. Why didn't she look up her classmates? She probably thought she was too good for them, too. She was going to have to talk to Frances as soon as she had some time alone with her, to let her know she was getting off on the wrong foot. No doubt Bernadette would want someone to tell her if she was making a poor impression.

But there was no stopping the rising bile. The tea was of no use. Bernadette pulled the wastebasket close and heaved. Oh God have mercy, she couldn't do months of this, please let it not be the whole trimester, please, let this be the end. She heaved and shuddered over the bin. And God, please help get rid of the fucking houseguest.

Jimmy lay in bed. Good thing he hadn't been sleeping because the goddamn racket the girls made would have woken him up. Chairs banging, raised voices. He'd probably get up to an awful mess. If you'd asked him when they were little, he would have told you he expected them to both be married or nearly married by now, but neither girl seemed close.

Then he heard the retching. He crept out of bed and pressed his ear against the door. Bernie was barfing, but why in God's name did she stay in her room? Had she never heard of a toilet? A better father would go check on her, if he had any idea what to say.

He had no idea what to say.

He listened as Bernie shuffled down the hall to the bathroom. When he heard the door close behind her, he tiptoed across the hall to her room. No mess that he could see, but an awful stench. He opened the window to let in air, and when he turned to leave Bernadette was standing at the door, wastebasket dangling from her hand.

"Fresh air is as good as medicine," Jimmy said.

"Thanks."

Jimmy slipped past her, returned to his room and closed the door.

He had a bad case of the jitters. That news report he watched at supper – he knew it was just a drill and that you should prepare for disaster, but when he got into bed his brain slipped into high gear. He started thinking about his girls getting hit by a LRT or crashing while riding on a LRT (say it went off the rails), and then he realized there were still worse things. There were always worse things. And you can't prepare for disaster. If a guy was prepared for a disaster then there wouldn't be a disaster because he'd have mortgage insurance, or a job, or a savings account with money in it. And he shouldn't dwell on it, but he couldn't stop dwelling on it. There wasn't any exercise Jimmy could think of that could prepare a guy for disaster.

Team Sport

In 1993, not too long before he turned ten years old, Brandon Phoenix Murray refused to go to hockey practice. He didn't like the outfit.

"Well, son," Jimmy said, "you won't be safe if you don't wear the gear."

Brandon's eyes filled with tears. "It's too stiff."

"You like playing hockey?"

Brandon nodded, then shook his head. "I don't like hockey," he whispered.

"No?"

Brandon shook his head.

"Your mom really wants you to play hockey."

"I'm not very good," he whispered.

"Well, that's not the only point of playing on a team."

"Yes it is."

Jimmy nodded. "Okay," he sighed. "I'll figure out something to tell your mom. But you're going to have to go to bed before she gets home."

"Okay!"

Jimmy waved at his grandson. "Go on up to your room. I need some time to think." Brandon skipped across the floor and up the stairs. The kid was a free spirit. Or something. And Jimmy was struck again with missing Frankie. She might have been a good friend to Brandon. He hadn't been right to let her go and it sat like a rock in his gut.

But dwelling on Frankie wasn't going to help Brandon. So, he would just hand it to Bernadette straight that Brandon didn't like playing hockey and, Jesus knew, Jimmy would be happy as hell not to drag his ass out of bed for 7:00 a.m. hockey practice. Bernadette would just have to cope, because that's what you did as a parent: you coped. And if she bitched about the registration fees, he'd pay her back. They'd have no problem selling the boy's equipment.

Jimmy took Brandon's backpack off its hook to clean out wrappers and make sure they weren't missing any teacher communications. He pulled out a sheet, a penciled sketch of a skinny bird with large wings standing on top of flames – a phoenix, of course. Jimmy had a small collection of phoenix drawings that Brandon had given him since starting school, but this was the best so far. Jimmy put the drawing in the back of the *Yellow Pages*. He'd grab it tomorrow and make a little template with it, to cut a bird out of that brown paisley he'd found in a remnants basket. He'd make Brandon a little quilted phoenix wall hanging for Christmas, from his own art. It would make the kid happier than a set of Hot Wheels.

And maybe Bernadette would get him into some kind of art class. There was no point in pushing him toward hockey or whatever else the kid hated. If Bernadette fought him on it, Jimmy would fight back. He'd bring up Frankie's name if he had to, because life had a way of bringing you back to your sins and making you look at them all over again. The joke was on him and Bernie, whether she realized it yet or not. And one day, when Brandon was old enough to understand, maybe Jimmy would try to tell him. He'd say to the boy, even when you think you're doing right, things aren't so cut and dry. He would tell him to take it easy because there are some things that you can't take back.

Kitchen Creations

The thing was, they were like three separate planets orbiting around anything but each other. Their dad was a total basket case, Europe had turned Frankie into a snob and Bernadette wanted them to be closer but didn't know how to unite them again as a family. The answer, she finally decided, was Thanksgiving dinner, impromptu as it was.

It came to her in a flash on Saturday: if nobody acted as though they were happy then nobody would be happy. Naturally it followed that if nobody acted as though they were thankful nobody could see that, regardless of what had gone down, they were still fucking lucky to have what they did. And so she went to Safeway and bought a ham and potatoes, Brussels sprouts, whipped cream and a pumpkin pie from the bakery – just a few things to be grateful for.

She wasn't going to let herself be brought down by lousy attitudes, either. Frankie and her friend slept more than half the day away and Jimmy had been holed up in his workroom, sewing, sewing, sewing. She didn't even want to know what. And the first thing

Robyn says is "Frankie's a vegetarian, you know." Well, actually, no she didn't know. Frankie had been eating everything she cooked and everything she cooked involved meat. She was trying to be nice to Robyn, in memory of Ken Oliver, rest in peace, but it seemed like Robyn's only goal was to be a pain in the ass, and once again she couldn't help but wonder how Ken had put up with the little brat.

"It's okay," Frances said. "I eat meat sometimes."

"Not that ham is really meat," Robyn said.

"Let's say grace," Bernadette said.

Jimmy lifted his head from his plate, "Good food, good meat, good God let's eat." He jammed his fork into his scalloped potatoes.

"Ha, ha, ha," Bernadette muttered.

"Bless us, oh Lord, and these, Thy gifts, which through Your bounty we are about to receive through Christ our Lord, amen," Frances said.

"A-men!" Robyn raised her arms like a bible thumper.

Jimmy stuffed potatoes into his mouth. "Yum, yum," he said.

Small steps were better than none. "We need to do this every week," Bernie said. "Sunday dinner."

"Sure," Frances replied.

Jimmy poured some more rye over what was left of his ice.

"That way we can keep up on what we're all doing." Bernadette was thinking of the baby now, how it would benefit from a family tradition like Sunday dinner.

"Hey, Mr. Murray, do you mind if I have some of your rye?"

Jimmy pushed the bottle toward Robyn. "Call me Jimmy."

"Thanks, Jimmy!"

"And then later on," Bernie said to Frances, "when we all live in our own places, we can still meet for dinners."

"You mean, like in Vancouver?" Robyn said.

"What?" Bernadette said.

"You don't expect she's going to just stay here in Calgary? A person like Frances can't spend her life in Calgary."

"What's your drift?"

Frances intervened. "Nothing. She's just making a joke. Of course I can spend my life in Calgary."

"But why would you want to?" Robyn said.

Jimmy took a swig from his rye. "This town's been good to me. It's those assholes in Ottawa I got a gripe with."

Robyn flicked her finger against her tumbler, listening for the ping of the crystal.

Bernadette snatched Robyn's glass from the table. "Stop that!"

"Whoa," Robyn said.

Bernadette set the drink back down. "You'll break the crystal."

"Jesus, Bernie," Frances said.

"I just want to have a nice meal," Bernie said.

Robyn placed her hand atop Bernadette's. "It's a really nice meal." Then she winked at Frances.

What the fuck did she wink at Frances for? "Thank you," Bernadette said. "There's pumpkin pie for dessert."

After they cleared the dishes Frankie and Robyn returned to the basement. While Jimmy was sleeping it off in his room, Bernadette regurgitated pretty much the entire contents of her meal, this time with the sink running in case Jimmy wasn't actually passed out. Then she sat on the side of the tub breathing heavily. The worst thing about taking the high road was no one knew you were taking the fucking high road. Bernadette sighed, stood up and rinsed her face.

Player

"Hey, I didn't know you were a Trooper fan." Robyn placed the album on the turntable and carefully dropped the needle onto the vinyl.

"It's from my dad. He was trying to be cool."

Robyn danced over to the couch and pulled a bottle out from under the sofa. She raised her arms over her head and danced to "We're Here for a Good Time."

"Where did you get that?"

"Oh, I have my ways, Frankie."

"I thought you were broke."

"My bank account is small, but my bag is big."

"What if you'd been caught?"

Robyn shrugged. "I wasn't. Be cool." She took a swig from the bottle then held it toward Frances.

"No thanks."

"Because you're here for a long time not a good time?"

"Ha ha ha," Frances said dryly.

Robyn ground her hips against Frances. "Let's have some fun." She waved the bottle in the air. "Come on, Frankie. Let's get shit-faced."

Frances took a swallow. "It tastes awful."

"Next time I'll get my hands on some Coke."

"Next time how about we don't drink at all?"

"Don't you want me to let go of my inhibitions?"

Frances laughed. "You have inhibitions?"

"One or two," Robyn said. "Now, let's get drunk and fool around."

Frances should have known better than to drink vodka like that. Her head was thumping and her eyes burned like mad. It was hard to believe that Tomas actually thought getting her to chop all the onions and garlic in the world was going to help her, but he was the boss and it was his right to enjoy a coffee and the crossword while she was in the kitchen chopping onions to oblivion.

Frances put her knife down and searched for some Tylenol. She could hear Reena's voice in her head: Don't do it, Frannie. Don't get mixed up with a straight girl. But maybe if there were such a thing as soulmates Robyn was hers. Maybe they were here for a good time *and* a long time. Why not? Why couldn't that happen to her?

Tomas pushed through the door.

Frances held up the bottle of pills. "Last night's vodka," she said, "and raw onions. Not a good mix."

Tomas wagged his finger at Frances. "My little brother thinks you're pretty special."

"I think Oscar's cool, too."

"Just don't let him think you're more than friends."

"Gawd, Tomas. As if."

"I'm just saying. Be very clear with Oscar. I mean I know that even if he weren't slow, he wouldn't be your type. But he doesn't know you have a type. Shit, he doesn't even know about your type."

"My type?"

"I'm not a bloody idiot, Frances."

"Okay."

"I'm not judging," Tomas said. "I don't get it. I think it's weird. But I'm not judging."

"If you say so."

"I never should have hired you."

"What?"

"Don't get all hurt. I mean I don't have the money."

Frances stopped chopping. "Great."

"I'm just trying to be honest here."

Frances nodded.

"But we're going to run this place until we can't. If you want to stick it out with us."

"Sounds good."

Tomas nodded.

Frances nodded.

"Now you go manage the front. I can't stand it out there. Tell Oscar if it gets busy, he's got to come back and wash dishes."

"Sure thing, boss." Because Frances liked these guys, and even though a smart person would look for another job, she was going to hang out here and worry about a new job when this one was actually gone.

Oscar was waiting for her with the checkerboard set up. "You want to be red or black?" he said.

Frances glanced around the room; the bar's regulars, Eugene, Betty and Louis, were at their usual table with a full jug of beer. Another guy sat against the wall rolling a smoke and nursing something with ginger ale in it. It was going to be a long night. Frances moved her first piece forward. "Red. Best out of three. No crying when I kick your butt."

"Ha! You'll be the one crying!" Oscar said.

"Just take your move, wise guy."

Oscar waved his hand across the board, trying to decide which piece to move as though a stupid game of checkers had life and death consequences.

Religion in Life

Sunday Mass was a quiet business at eight in the morning, less than half full, populated by small clusters of old folks scattered across the pews. Father Mark led the mass, flanked by lethargic altar boys. Jimmy, with no real conviction, declared, "I confess to almighty God, and to you, my brothers and sisters, that I have sinned through my own fault in my thoughts and in my words, in what I have done, and what I have failed to do; and I ask the blessed Mary, ever virgin, and all the angels and saints, and you my brothers and sisters, to pray for me to the Lord, our God."

Jimmy dropped onto the pew while the rest of the congregation remained standing. He confessed weekly and prayed more than that, but mostly as a way of staying close to Doris. Maybe he went about things wrong. Maybe there was a way to pray so that things turned out better. Maybe if he'd had a vocation and taken up orders. He might have been well suited to the life of a priest – three squares a day, free wine. Also, no twenty-one percent mortgage, no getting fired from your job, no Visa bill, no goddamn bills at all, no clean-ing up after yourself, no shovelling the snow, no mowing the lawn, no kids, no wife, no banging emptiness, no waking up every day to nothing left.

Jimmy sighed. He was probably romanticizing it. Doris had lost her connection to God in the convent and found it (so she said) again in his house. But if Doris had been a priest, top of the heap, she might never have left – everybody kissing your ass, now that would keep you close to God. Busy two days a week, and then a little bit of this and a little bit of that for the rest of your time. Yessir, Jimmy could've got used to that, even with the celibacy. Jimmy was living proof that there were harder things in life than celibacy.

He stood for the Alleluia, shook his body out and nodded his head in silent apology to Doris for letting his mind wander while in Mass. Then he offered a second silent prayer to Barb, whose mem-ory couldn't compete with Doris's. But Doris and Jimmy had been friends in a way he never found with Barb (rest in peace) because those early days with little kids were all about the work. And they were broke and flat-out tired. Maybe if Barb had lived, they'd have ended up happy as clams. Or mad as hell at each other. He'd seen it both ways, though more often the second than the first.

Well, he was through with all that now – two dead wives was more than enough for a strong man, and Jimmy never claimed to be that.

"This is the Gospel of the Lord," Father said.

Jimmy closed his eyes and tried to recall what it was like to have Doris standing next to him. The subtle rose scent from her soap floating toward him, her hand brushing against his, her attention, her belief. And his delight to be standing next to her.

"Praise to you, Lord Jesus Christ," Jimmy said.

Attendance

Robyn was still wearing last night's black dress; her mascara had been reduced to dark shadows under her eyes. The basement was ripe with the stench that radiated from her: stale booze, cigarette smoke and some sharp, cheap cologne. She held an unlit cigarette between her lips and swayed to The Police.

Frances watched her dad unfold and measure a rectangle of fabric. Robyn had been out all night and Frances was doing her best to not cry, to stay cool.

The song ended and Robyn opened her eyes. "Do you have a light?"

Frances pointed to a lighter on the coffee table.

"I think I'm still drunk," Robyn said.

"Smells like it," Frances said. She turned toward the stairs. "Gotta go. See you, Dad."

Jimmy cut carefully through the fabric. He gave no indication of having heard Frances.

"Are you angry with me?" Robyn asked.

Frances stopped and look at Robyn. "Should I be?"

"You're my best friend, Frankie."

Frances breathed deeply and nodded. "Good to know."

"Friendship is better than love."

"My dad is right here!"

"In body only. I'd like some of what he's on."

"Seriously, Robyn? Do you not think of anyone else in this room? Ever?"

"Whoa. You need to relax."

"You need to not trivialize everything."

"How do you feel about Elvis?"

"What?"

"I was thinking we could go as Elvis and Priscilla this Halloween."

"If you knew anything about me, you'd know I fucking hate Halloween."

"That's not even natural," Robyn said.

"And, as you well know, I'm not natural." Frances turned on her heel and marched upstairs.

Bernadette was heating some broth on the stove. She watched Frances lace her boots.

"That little friend of yours sure gets around," Bernadette said.

"I guess so."

"I hope she doesn't get herpes."

Frances looked at her sister. "Are you for real, Bernie?"

"Well you got to admit, she's pretty loose. What do you think Doris would say about her?"

"That she who is without sin cast the first stone."

"I'm not casting a stone. I'm just stating the facts."

"Wow. Do you try to be an asshole or does it just come naturally to you?"

"Calm yourself," Bernadette said. "I can't be saying anything you haven't noticed."

"Blow it out your ass," Frances said and slammed out the door.

NAMES TO FULLER

Tasty Treats

Frances was at work chopping onions again (because you could never have enough onions) while Robyn was at home in the basement sleeping it off. It made her crazy that she had stayed awake all night worrying, even though she knew – she knew for sure that Robyn had picked up some guy and hadn't come to any harm. But she'd lain there all night freaking out. Because Robyn dead or Robyn screwing some guy were pretty much equally awful.

Well, obviously it was worse if Robyn was dead. Much worse. Frances blew out a gust of air and wiped her burning eyes.

After her break, after she'd polished off a medium ham and pineapple pizza, it seemed a little foolish to stay angry. What they should do is have a talk, and Frances should just put it all out there, her real feelings for Robyn. Except she didn't want to be that clingy person. And she didn't want to embarrass herself. And she really didn't want to be the jealous type.

"Hungover?" Tomas asked.

"No."

"You haven't said three words tonight. And you packed that pizza away."

Frances shook her head. "I'm just tired."

Tomas nodded. "Clean out the walk-in when you finish with those pots, and then you can go."

"I can stay."

"Your pal called to ask when you were off. I told her I was sending you home."

"Great," she said dryly.

"Hey, don't let me be the guy who interferes with girl plans."

Robyn was waiting in the basement when Frances got home. She'd prepared a plate of peanut butter sandwiches cut into neat triangles. The plate sat in the centre of the coffee table, next to a jug of grape Kool-Aid. Robyn held up a box of Cap'n Crunch. "Dessert," she said.

Despite herself, Frances smiled.

"I'm sorry, Frankie. I should have called you."

Frances shrugged.

"I was just too drunk to come home."

"I'm sorry, too," Frances said. "Things are just weird, you know, with Dad, and Doris. Even Bernie is being weird."

"I made a gourmet meal."

"I noticed."

"I even have some vodka."

"None for me."

"Then none for me either."

Frances smiled again. "I'm just going to throw on my sweats."

While Frances was changing, Robyn unscrewed the vodka cap and took a big swig directly from the bottle, then poured a large measure into her cup and covered it with Kool-Aid. She filled Frances's glass with the juice and passed it to her when she returned.

Robyn raised her cup. "To us," she said.

"To us." Frances reached for a peanut butter triangle.

Outdoors in The City

Robyn found a massive brown wig at Value Village and a wedding dress with yellow stains at the armpits. She looked more bride of Frankenstein than Priscilla Presley but, apparently, that was the fun of Halloween. Frances would rather be at work, but Robyn had cajoled and whined until she booked the night off.

Frances examined herself in the mirror. She'd let Robyn spray her hair black and smother it with goop. She looked more like a creepy undercover cop than Elvis, but Robyn had trekked to the Old Y to buy dance tickets then engaged in a relentless hunt for the perfect costumes, and Frances liked her look. She was dressed in a dark grey man's suit with a snap-on bowtie and ill-fitting Oxfords. Frances could see herself in the suit again, only with her Docs instead of the uncomfortable shoes. "You're a handsome bloke," she told the mirror.

But when her dad saw her, he walked right over and touched her hair. "Jesus, kid," he said.

Bernadette was more direct: "Don't go all lesbian on us."

They were on their way to the Womyn's Collective dance, a first for Frances. On the walk to the bus, Robyn said, "I scored us some mushrooms."

"Not a chance."

"It'll be fun!"

"For you maybe."

"Suit yourself." Robyn popped a gelatin capsule filled with ground psilocybin onto her tongue. "Don't blame me if I have more fun than you."

"You were always going to have more fun than me," Frances muttered.

Robyn was quiet on the bus down to Bridgeland, but as they walked into the dance she whispered in Frances's ear, "I'm starting to trip." She kissed Frances on the cheek. "You grab us a beer and I'll find us a place to sit," she said, and twirled away into the crowd, the top of her bouffant wig bouncing.

The community hall was set up with long tables, each covered in black plastic. Orange and black ribbons were strung across the low ceiling and wound around two pillars that framed the entryway. Paper spiders were strung from the ceiling. A country tune was playing; rancher and trucker types dressed as superheroes, or witches, or spiders, or bunnies two-stepped across the floor. The punks, teachers and university students, also dressed as superheroes, witches, spiders or bunnies, were mostly sitting out the country tune. A tall woman, dressed as a cowboy but not in costume, pulled Robyn onto the dance floor. The cowboy said something and Robyn threw her head back and laughed dramatically. Jesus.

Frances put down ten bucks and picked up five beer tickets. Against the wall, a pirate and skeleton were passionately making out. Beers in hand, she turned to the dance floor: Robyn and the cowboy were still shaking it up, now to Kool & the Gang. Frances guzzled her beer then returned to their coats. She dug the second capsule out of Robyn's jacket and popped it. What the fuck. Then she parked herself against the wall and waited for Robyn to return.

Robyn found Frances in the toilet. Frances felt a hand tugging on the heel of her shoe.

"Frankie?"

Frances lifted her head from the toilet. "Yeah."

"I've been looking for you for hours." Robyn climbed onto the toilet in the next stall and hung over the top. "You're puking?"

"More or less, I'm just resting now."

"Bummer."

Frances looked at her watch. "Anyway, I've only been in the can for twenty minutes."

"You didn't get us a table."

"You were dancing."

"I wanted to dance with you."

"You did all right without me."

"Well, I know how to make the best out of a bad situation."

Frances pushed herself up and spit into the toilet.

"It's one of my better qualities," Robyn said.

Frances stepped out of her stall and Robyn jumped down to join her. "I was looking for you to see if you wanted to go outside. It's too tight in here."

More than anything Frances wanted to get the fuck out of there. "I still have beer tickets."

Robyn plucked them from her hands and tucked them into the mirror frame. "Now someone else can use them."

There was no going back to the house. Not in their condition. So Frances and Robyn made their way across the river, toward Ninth and the southeast. The night was mild and they walked slowly. When they reached Colonel Walker school they cut across the yard and tucked themselves in against the darkened walls of the old building.

"Remind me never to do mushrooms again," Frances sunk to the ground.

"If I'm around."

"You're going?"

"Well. Not right this minute."

Frances nodded. "When?"

Robyn flopped down beside Frances and pulled her wig off. She flung it away. The wig rose on a gust of wind and sailed across the field.

Frances, struck by the tumbleweed of flying hair, burst into laughter.

"Magic carpet ride," Robyn shouted and Frances laughed harder.

Robyn rolled on top of Frances, pressed her back onto the grass and kissed her. Frances stopped laughing. She lay still and let Robyn move her mouth down her body. She let the thoughts of Robyn's potential leaving drift away and focused instead on the pleasure at hand. Whatever they were in this moment, it was enough.

Scribe

Frannie,

I was very happy to find your letter waiting at home. Sorry for the slow reply. To be very honest, I've had to take some time to think about just what I wanted to write to you.

I suppose I foolishly hoped that you and I would find a way to stay together despite the fact that we are on separate continents. It is true that I love you, but it is also true that I wish for you to find happiness, even if it doesn't involve me. I know that I have said it is mad to date a straight woman, but who's to say that it won't work out for you? So, with that in mind, I am writing to wish you every happiness.

And it sounds like your family is pleased to have you back, really. Don't you know all older sisters are bossy? It is the nature of families, I think, that we older siblings "guide" our younger counterparts. You call it bossy, we call it affection! Honestly, I think you just have to adjust to one another again.

As for me, I'm going to visit the women at the Greenham Peace Camp. Is it being covered on your news? They're protesting the cruise missiles and this whole terrifying nuclear thing. It seems pressing, to say the least and I want to feel like I'm doing something.

Please don't feel like you must continue to write to me. I have no idea how long I will be at the camp, nor do I know when or how I would even get your letters.

Do take care, and please be happy.

With much affection,
Reena

Robyn folded the letter and placed it back in its envelope on Frankie's bedside table. Reena was the kind of chick she would one hundred percent hate: a self-righteous dyke. Frankie (or, she should say, Frannie) was lucky to be rid of her.

She lit a smoke and sank into the bed, pinched her stockings with her toes and pulled them toward her. With her cigarette gripped tightly between her lips she pulled her stockings on. There was a tear in the knee she had no memory of making. Whatever. Robyn set her smoke on the edge of the coffee table, wiggled into a miniskirt and pulled on a see-through blouse she'd found at the Sally Ann. She wore a red bra underneath. Perfect.

Robyn was on her way to Bar None – to see Frankie, but Tomas would be around, too – and she would be a liar if she didn't say she had a thing for his receding hairline and soft little belly. She liked the way he checked her out – not like some dirty old horndog, but he wasn't afraid of just directly looking at her. Feeling Tomas's eyes on her lit Robyn up, made her feel like her hips were made of butter. What was the harm in feeling so good when most things had gone to shit?

Weather

Bernadette hadn't been able to shake the thought, ever since Robyn had mentioned it, that Frankie wasn't the kind of person who could spend the rest of her life in Calgary. Because, first of all, anybody could spend all of their life anywhere. She'd tried talking to Jimmy about it, asked him if he thought there was something off about Robyn, but he just shook his head.

"You have too much time on your hands," Jimmy said. "If you've got the time to worry about the habits of that girl, you need to take on a hobby."

"What about Frankie?"

"Seems fine to me. She's got a job."

Of course he would say that. He'd always let Frankie get away with murder. Bernadette watched her dad at the sewing machine; he was working on some kind of blanket. But he was totally out of it. He clearly hadn't noticed Frankie moping around when Robyn stayed out all night. If he had, he might have a different opinion about Robyn and he might show a little more concern for Frankie, who could very well be headed down a wrong path. It was sickening. Sickening.

In future years, Bernadette would think back to this conversation with Jimmy and how she'd known. She'd known, but did nothing to stop it. She didn't blame herself; that would be absurd. Frankie had made adult choices and realized adult consequences. But maybe Bernadette should have taken a firmer hand in things and maybe Frankie shouldn't have been left to her own devices for so many years.

Bernadette didn't take responsibility, but she did worry for Frankie's soul. As late as 2006 Bernadette was praying for Frankie, for her return to virtue. She spoke to Father Joe and to her Tuesday night prayer group, and they all prayed, but to no avail. There was never a meaningful word from Frankie – whatever communication they had was terse at best, and if Bernadette were really honest, she would say it pissed her right off. What made Frankie think she was so frigging special that she could just cut people out?

Then on June 23, 2006, over afternoon cocktails on a sunny patio, Brandon said three things.

The first, and most hurtful, was, "Don't you think she might keep away because of you?" Because she thought she was there to enjoy her son's company, the fair weather and a gin and tonic.

The second was that he wished to be called Phoenix, not Brandon. But she was already reeling and couldn't even point out how it was a joke, a hormonal glitch, that she'd given him that name at all. What kind of a job would he get with a name like Phoenix?

And then he said, "I am in love with Sam."

She asked, "Samantha?"

And he said, "Very funny, Mom, but I swear if you're a bitch you'll never see me again either."

Strong women are always called bitch, she wanted to say, but she kept her mouth shut. And she didn't pray for her sister again after that. Not once.

In the late fall of 1983, she was still trying to keep things together. She tried to warn her dad, but he was hell-bent on not seeing what he didn't want to see. He ignored the mess and so then did she. It's not like they didn't have enough to worry about already; it was a perfect shitstorm.

Child Care

Frances slipped out of bed, careful not to wake Robyn, who was sleeping deeply, her mouth slightly open, air sputtering between her lips, not quite a snore. Frances had been nearly asleep but was jolted awake at the recollection of a comment Rita had made earlier that evening. "You know what makes me laugh?" Rita said. She was in a mood after two guys who'd polished off a couple of pints dashed out, leaving their bill unpaid. Fuckers.

"No," Frances answered. She was busy stacking ashtrays under the bar, trying to avoid the storm.

"The way your little friend is working on my old man. You might warn her to watch herself." Rita shook her head. "She must think I'm blind." Then she laughed, meanly. "She must think she's the first."

"Robyn's just a little over the top," Frances said.

"You could do better."

Frances blushed and shrugged. "Do what better?"

Rita snorted. "Oh, for Christ's sake. You know exactly what I'm talking about." She lit a cigarette. "Go tell Oscar to bring me a bowl of ice cream, would you? Tell him he can sit down and have a float with me if he likes."

When Frances was alone with Tomas, she tested him. She looked at the watch on her wrist then at Tomas. "Robyn will be here soon."

"Oh yeah?"

"It's cool with you that she hangs around?"

"As long as she pays for her drink."

Frances nodded. "For sure."

And she let it go, because Tomas spent no more than five minutes out front after Robyn arrived and, anyway, Rita had been in a terrible mood for the past couple of weeks and she and Tomas had been bickering pretty much non-stop. Of course Rita was going to look for someone to blame for the lousy situation they were in.

After work Robyn took off her clothes and waited in the bed for Frances. They made out and it was great – it was always great. And just as they were drifting into sleep Robyn said, "Your boss is kind of hot."

"He's married," Frances said. "He's old."

"I know." Robyn pressed her back into Frances. "I was just saying." And it seemed like it was nothing because she fell right asleep. Frances almost fell asleep, too, until she recalled Rita's snarky comments.

She padded upstairs to take a pee, rolling Robyn's words over in her head. Tomas and Rita were a happy couple in their own weird way. And they were pretty old, thirty at least. Frances saw all sorts of people who were cute and she never acted on it. There was no reason to think Robyn was any different. Actually, there were lots of reasons to think Robyn was different, but things had been going so smoothly between them and Robyn hadn't been out all night in almost three weeks. Frances couldn't help but believe that things were moving forward and they were becoming a proper couple.

When she came out of the bathroom Bernadette was standing at the door with her arms crossed. She pushed past Frances and closed the door.

"Nice," Frances said.

Bernadette didn't respond. Frances headed back to the basement but stopped when she heard Bernie throw up. She held her breath and listened while her sister puked. She thought of leaving when she heard the taps running, but what if Bernie wanted help? She waited.

When Bernadette opened the door and spied her sister, she put up her hand. "Don't say a fucking word," she said.

"Are you okay?"

"What did I just say?"

Frances sighed. "Do you always have to be such a hard-ass?"

"You can put the kettle on," Bernadette said. "But I don't want to talk about it."

Frances passed Bernie a weak cup of tea laced with milk and sugar. "This should help."

"Thanks."

Frances leaned against the counter. "What's up, Bern?"

Bernie shot her an icy look. "Nothing for you to worry about."

"Who said I was worried?" Frances said.

Bernadette relented. "I'm going to be sick for months."

Frances clapped her hands. "You're knocked up!"

"Do not tell a soul," Bernadette hissed.

"So then you're keeping it?"

"What's your point?"

"No point," Frances said, "I'm asking if you're going to keep it."

"Of course I'm going to keep it!"

"Because, you know, you could –" Frances waved her hand. "Terminate."

"Not in your fucking life."

"Again. Just asking." Frances took a chair next to Bernadette. "So, when do we meet the dad?"

Bernadette snorted. "He's dead."

"That's awful."

Bernadette shook her head. "Not especially."

"Jesus, Bernie, that's just cold."

Bernadette shrugged. "Honestly, it's no big deal. Auntie."

Frances smiled. "Auntie," she said, "wow."

Frances crawled back into bed and nuzzled close to Robyn. For the first time since she got back to Calgary she felt good about being here. A baby could be fun. She and Robyn could take the baby for sleepovers when Bernie needed a break. And, if her dad kept it up, he could sew the baby clothes. She swallowed a giggle; the idea of her dad at the sewing machine, making little baby clothes was a bit much. But then, who was she to judge?

Law Awareness

 Bernadette couldn't exactly remember the dream, but in it she had a pressing urge to speak to Frankie. She had to lay down the law, make Frankie understand that it was imperative she keep her trap shut.

She swung her legs out of bed.

Bernadette would tell soon enough, but right now, while her body adjusted, while she barfed her guts out, while she accustomed herself to the idea of being an actual mother and not just a pregnant girl, she wanted to keep it to herself. She wanted to keep it to herself, turn it around and admire it on her own terms. Why had she said anything? She needed Frankie to say nothing, not even to her. This was Bernie's time, the secret time when only she and the baby knew about each other. When no one else could talk, judge or otherwise fuck up her day. She didn't want this ruined. And she didn't want Frankie to screw it up.

Frances woke up to Bernadette standing above her bed.

"What the fuck, Frankie?" Bernadette hissed.

Robyn had turned around in the night and lodged herself tightly under Frances's arm.

"What?" Frances asked.

"What if Dad came downstairs?" She waved her arm over the tangle of their bodies.

"He would knock?"

Robyn stirred.

"We're just sleeping," Frances said. "And it's cold down here."

"Just sleeping naked?"

Frances pushed herself up on her elbow. "Don't you think you're overreacting?"

"Don't you think you should show Dad a little more respect?"

"Who died and made you Mother Teresa?"

"I can't believe that just because you've been living in Europe all free and easy you think you have the right to come back here and flaunt your lifestyle under our noses. Actions have consequences, Frankie."

"What's Dad going to say when he finds out you're knocked up?"

"Pregnancy is natural!"

Robyn, eyes still closed, began to shake with laughter.

"Have some dignity," Bernadette said.

"You're not serious?" Frances began to laugh, too.

"You're the one who's not serious," Bernadette said. "I can't believe your nerve. And you're lucky I don't tell Dad because he'd throw you out on your ass." She turned and marched out of the basement.

"Would he really?" Robyn said.

"What?"

"Throw you out."

"No," Frances said. Then she shook her head. "I don't know."

"I don't think he would," Robyn said.

Frances nodded. She hadn't really considered her dad before. What he thought of her. What he would think of her if he knew. A ball of anxiety tightened in her gut.

Robyn turned toward Frances. "I don't think he'd care," Robyn muttered against her neck. "Anyway, we're just having fun. I don't know why she had to make such a big deal."

Frances pulled out of Robyn's arms and stood up. "Yeah," she said, not at all confident that her dad wouldn't care, and even less convinced that she was just having fun.

Frances read the note that her sister tossed into the basement: *Shut up or else!* She wasn't entirely clear what Bernie expected her to be quiet about – if she was talking about her own pregnancy or about Robyn. Well, she would keep her mouth shut about Bernie, and she figured Bernadette would keep her mouth shut, too. Mutually assured destruction. It didn't just work for Reagan.

Except that once it was in her mind – what her dad would say if he knew she was a lesbian – it ate at Frances. Would he throw her out on her ass? Maybe Bernie was right, maybe he would. She'd never really thought of him as one of those parents, but how the hell would she know unless she said something?

Reena said her mom had refused to acknowledge her coming out, that she still suggested boys who she thought could be potential husbands. Frances could cope with something like that, some kind of stubborn disbelief. But what would she do if her dad got angry – if, all of sudden, he hated her? She couldn't shake the feeling that she should know what her dad felt, no matter what Bernie had written in her stupid note.

Reporting

Jimmy had the Remembrance Day ceremony on. The mother of the fallen soldier – eighty-five if she was a day – carefully placed a wreath at the base of the war memorial. Her two daughters, now old women themselves, stood beside her, all three of them weighed down by their black overcoats, by their losses. And the line of veterans back in uniform for the day, grim faced. Oh, he could just imagine what was going through their heads. He thought of his uncle Gordon, home from the First World War and never really right again, living in the back room at Jimmy's grandmother's and talking to no one.

Then he screwed up his goddamn square with all the feelings he was feeling watching the bloody TV and was left pulling out stitches. Again.

Frankie walked into the living room and flopped onto the couch. She sighed loudly, stood up then flopped back onto the couch again with her head at the other end. "Hi," she said.

Jimmy held his finger to his lips and then pointed to the television.

"Right," she said. "Our annual celebration of sanctioned murder."

"Judas Priest," Jimmy muttered.

"Sorry." Frances jumped up and stood in the window. The uncharacteristically grey sky was beginning to clear. "It's still pretty cloudy," she said.

Jimmy, pointedly, didn't answer. He picked up his remote control – an old broomstick with a notch he'd carved into its bottom end – fitted it over the top dial and turned up the volume.

Frances leaned her forehead against the glass, sighed heavily then turned and flopped back down on the couch.

The kid was flipping around like a fish out of water. "Sit still, would you?" He sounded rougher than he meant to.

Frances sat up. She pinched her hands between her knees. "Dad, I'm a lesbian." She said it so fast he could barely make out the words.

Jimmy chewed on his lips and continued to stare at the TV. Doris had suggested as much when Frankie went off to England, but he'd just laughed. Doris had laughed, too, then said, "I've met more than one lesbian in my life and I'm telling you, I'm pretty sure."

"But not a hundred percent certain?" Jimmy had asked, and Doris agreed, not a hundred percent certain.

"You going to say anything?" Frankie asked him.

"Nope."

"Are you mad?"

"No, Frankie." Jimmy could feel a first-rate headache coming on. He dropped the yarn and crochet needle into his lap.

"I just wanted you to know," she said.

Jesus, did every blessed little thing have to be talked about? She took a breath, "I want you to know who I am. For real."

Jimmy nodded. He wasn't going to say a frigging word. Nothing good could come out of him speaking right now. He nodded again, to himself mostly.

"I don't want to lie to you."

Jesus, Mary and Joseph. "Frankie," he said.

"I couldn't stand it if you hated me." Her voice broke. "Well, I could stand it, but I'd hate it if you hated me."

"I don't hate you." Jimmy pulled his fingers down his nose, pinching his nostrils and releasing them.

"Okay." Frances stood up. "Thanks, Dad."

"Don't go thanking me."

"Some people won't talk to their kids."

Jimmy nodded at Frankie. "Now I'm concentrating on this here." He held up the square. "So off you go."

Jimmy could feel Frankie's eyes on him, but he kept his head down in a pose of pure concentration. He didn't want to answer questions right now, not about his needlework and sure as hell not about his daughter's taste in people, or whatever you wanted to call it. He kept his eyes on his work until he felt her leave the room.

Angler

How do you even know you're gay? How do you know you're not just confused? That's what Bernadette really wanted to say to Frankie. Also: if you're looking for a mother figure you could have done better. But she kept her lips zipped.

And really, Frankie mostly never had a mother. Now Bernadette's job was to help her see that. That was the angle she would take, to show Frankie that her behaviour wasn't really her fault because she'd mostly never had a mother. Of course she would easily be led astray, especially by people like Robyn.

If Bernie thought back to herself at twenty, well she'd had problems, too. She was still wandering around Toronto then, no friends to speak of, except for a few boyfriends. Not that she was a slut – she wasn't having any fun – and she was just so alone. All Frankie needed was some guidance, some direction. Bernadette knew how it was to be aimless and she would have been so grateful if someone had stepped up for her. If someone had been on her side.

So Bernadette apologized to Frankie. She said it was the stress of everything lately, and Frankie said, "Yeah I know, it's been crazy." And that was that. Because Bernadette wanted to help Frankie sort things out, so that everyone would be happier.

She didn't apologize to Robyn because, really, that was just too much. Robyn grated on Bernadette. Ken would be broken-hearted by his daughter, pulling up her skirts for anyone, male or female. These days, when business was bad enough to destroy Ken's company, when the stress had been enough to kill her dad, all Robyn wanted to do was party. She was an embarrassment and it was just as well that her dad wasn't around to see it.

Chemistry

"It's like, where I come from," Robyn slurred, "you just don't pull shit like that." She was wasted.

Frances had no idea what Robyn was talking about. She'd been in the kitchen cleaning up and prepping food. A half hour earlier, Tomas had just stopped in the middle of cleaning, tore off his apron and said, "Fuck this." He told Frances to close the kitchen and he walked out.

After that, Rita came in with a beer and said, "Your *friend* is here." She set the bottle forcibly against the steel counter. It clattered and foam spilled out the top.

Now Rita sat at the bar on the right side of Tomas, whose full attention was turned to Robyn sitting on his left. Rita looked bored or, more likely, angry. She was smoking a cigarette and thumbing through a copy of *Alberta Report* a customer had left behind.

"What's she talking about?" Frances asked.

"Fucking other women's husbands," Rita said.

"Really?"

"That's what she should be talking about." Rita crushed out her cigarette. "Who writes this shit?" She waved the magazine.

Frances shrugged.

"Some sob story about her mother, I think," Rita said. "Where I come from people don't talk about their mothers like that."

"Her mom is mean."

"I'd be mean, too. If she were my daughter."

Robyn brushed something, or nothing, off of Tomas's cheek. She let her hand linger a moment too long.

Frances looked back to Rita. "She's a good person."

Rita sucked her teeth. "Why don't you grab us another beer?"

"Frankie!" Robyn shouted when she saw Frances behind the bar. "She's my best friend." Robyn placed her hand on Tomas's arm.

Tomas nodded. "She's a hard worker."

"Hard is good," Robyn said then brought her hand back to support her chin.

"Tomas!" Rita said. "Go phone your brother. Make sure he's doing okay. Ask does he want me to bring him anything. A Kit Kat or some licorice."

Tomas pushed himself away from the bar. He began to dial and Rita lit another cigarette. The door opened and Rita shouted, "We're closed."

"I'm here to pick up Frances," Bernadette said.

Tomas put the phone down. "He wants some Nibs."

"Lock the door, for Christ's sake," Rita told Tomas. "So, you're the sister."

"Big. Bad. Bernadette," Robyn said.

"In the flesh," Bernadette answered.

"Tomas, get the girl a drink," Rita ordered.

Bernadette put up her hand. "Nothing for me, thanks." She sat down beside Frances.

"Is something wrong?" Frances asked.

"No."

"Alrighty."

"I thought I'd be nice. It's cold tonight."

"Okay."

"I'm pretty sure this is where you thank me."

Frances looked at her sister. "Thank you, Bernadette," she said slowly.

Bernadette smiled tightly then turned to Rita. "Nice place you've got here."

"You can have it," Rita said. "It's sucking us dry."

Robyn squealed with laughter.

"You better get your friend out of here before I murder her," Rita told Frances. Frances swallowed the last of her beer and stood up.

"So I'm not the only one," Bernadette said.

"Jesus Christ, Bernie, give it a break," Frances snapped.

"I'm just kidding!"

"Okay, time to go home now." Rita waved her hand at Robyn. "Off you go. Tomas, show the ladies out."

On the drive home, neither Frances nor Bernadette spoke.

"That was fun," Robyn said.

Bernadette shook her head. Frances stared out the window.

When they were alone in the basement, Frances said, "Rita thinks you're trying to screw her husband."

"Well, he is hot. I mean, in a rustic kind of way."

"He's my boss."

"He's not my boss."

"I can't believe you'd say that."

"Why are you so worked up?"

"I'm not worked up. I'm just telling you, Rita was not impressed."

"I don't give a shit about Rita."

"How about me? Maybe you could show some concern for me."

"I honestly don't get what you're upset about."

"It's just a little bit awkward to watch my girlfriend flirting with my boss. You get that at least?"

"I'm nobody's girlfriend."

Frances nodded. Then she nodded again. "Good to know," she said. She turned away from Robyn. "Goodnight."

Later, Robyn climbed into bed beside her, and Frances lay perfectly still and breathed deeply to give the impression that she was sleeping soundly, that she didn't have a care in the world.

Cycling

Jimmy opened his eyes to the dark room. He'd gone to sleep thinking of a farmland quilt. Yellow and brown squares, and some green, like sections. Maybe some white. Some kind of blue sky at the top. But again, he'd fallen into the dream where he is looking for Doris and she's gone. In this version of the dream Jimmy ran into the rumpus room, but it wasn't really the rumpus room – it was the garage and Brian was pouring water into the coffee maker, except Brian looked like Mike Wallace.

"Jimmy," Brian had said. "If everybody tried harder we could all have work. You have to try harder." Then Jimmy asked Brian if he'd seen Doris, but as soon as he spoke he flipped a tooth out with his tongue and then reached in and pulled out another tooth. And then Jimmy woke up. And while he lay there blinking, the weight of the day began to press into him.

He closed his eyes and listened to the sounds: the furnace kicking in, some fool dog in the distance barking like a maniac, a car driving up the street. It was early hours yet, but Jimmy had no hope of falling back to sleep. Every morning was the same: he woke too early and was full of regret, an endless cycle.

He curled his legs against his chest, turned his face into his pillow and began to cry. He was sick of the wide-ranging loneliness that blew through his life. He cried for missing Doris so badly. And he cried for Frankie's terrible news, because he didn't know how he could bear to repeat it to anyone, ever. He cried, too, because he could see his days set out ahead of him without promise. No wife, no work, nothing at all coming down the pike. Everything a blank page and not the kind you tell a kid is good and that they have their whole life ahead of them! Instead, Jimmy had a blank page where you look back at your own life and ask yourself, what the hell did I ever do but screw it all up?

You & Others

 Her dad ran out of the kitchen like he was prey and she was the hunter. Frances sighed and followed him into the living room.

"Hey, Dad, want to talk about it?"

"What?" Jimmy backed into his chair. "No. No, I don't want to talk. What are you talking about?"

"What I said to you. Do you want to talk about what I said to you?"

"All of a sudden you want to talk to me," Jimmy said.

"Actually, Dad, you haven't talked to me pretty much since I came out to you."

"Is that what you call it?"

"What do you call it?"

"I call it B.S."

Tears sprang to the corners of her eyes. "I just don't know how to pretend to be what I'm not," Frances said.

"And I just don't know how to pretend to be happy about it." He rubbed his eyes. "Your mother has got to be rolling in her grave," he muttered. "And your little friend, what does she have to say about it?"

"Dad ..." Frances slumped onto the couch. It was too much to explain. "She's fine with it."

"I don't know what to do, Frankie," he said. "If money wasn't so tight ..." He shook his head. "I don't know if I can get used to it. To what you said."

"You want me to move out?"

"Well now, that's easier said than done these days, isn't it?"

A ringing sounded in her head, shrill and behind her eyes. "Yup," Frances said. "But you'll be happy to know I'm off to pick up my cheque. So at least you'll get a few bucks for your trouble."

Jimmy watched her leave the room, his stomach churning with disappointment. He popped a cigarette in his mouth and lit it with shaking hands. What the fuck was he supposed to do, give her a prize?

So really, it was just the icing on the cake when Frances walked into the kitchen at Bar None and found Robyn, skirt hiked up to her waist and perched on the stainless steel counter, getting royally pounded by Tomas. Because it was already a shitty day, why not add to it?

Tomas reached her at the door. He grabbed her arm. "Frankie, stop."

She yanked her arm away. "Do not call me Frankie."

"Frances," he said. "We're just fooling around. Nothing serious."

"Tell that to Rita."

"True, Rita wouldn't like it. But it's just some fun, so no need to say anything."

"Really, Frankie. We're just burning off steam," Robyn said from the door of the kitchen.

"You." Frances pointed at Robyn. "Get your shit, and get the fuck out of my house. Today. And if you don't then Rita will hear about it, and I have no clue what will happen to Tomas but I'm pretty sure she'll slap the shit out of you."

"Frankie, you've got it all wrong –"

Frances cut her off. "Shut up, Robyn." She stuffed her paycheque into her back pocket. "Just get the fuck out of my house."

"Frankie, please."

"I am done with you." She turned to Tomas. "And you're fucking lucky I need this job, you pig."

She pushed through the door.

"Shit," Robyn muttered.

Frances stayed out until after supper to give herself time to cool down and so Robyn had time to clear out (she better have cleared out), and so she could think about what to say to her dad. Her head was aching from too much lousy coffee and the three donuts she'd had. She ran the tap for a glass of water.

Bernadette stomped into the kitchen and hissed, "I can't believe you told Dad. As if he hasn't had enough heartbreak already."

Frances turned the tap off and swallowed her water. "And that will be number three," she said.

"What?"

"Did Robyn leave?"

"Are you even listening to me?" Bernadette was seething.

Frances shook her head. "No, I'm not."

"You tell him something tomorrow. You tell him you're confused and you miss your mother. You tell him you need counselling."

"Why don't I just tell him he's going to be a grandpa, for real this time? That'll cheer him up."

Bernadette took a step toward Frances with her hand raised.

Frances laughed. "Come on, Bernie. I dare you. Give it your best shot."

Bernadette let her arm drop. "What is wrong with you? What is even going through that little head of yours?"

"Oh, I don't know, Bernadette. I just thought my family loved me and would accept me. No matter what."

"He is praying for you, Frankie. And he is heartbroken."

"Has it occurred to you I might have hurt feelings, too?"

"Oh, give me a break!" Bernadette said. "You know, I've had it up to here with everybody talking about their goddamn feelings. I mean, really, who gives a shit about your precious feelings? What about doing the right thing? What about just shutting up and doing the right thing? Why is it so important to reveal all the disgusting little details of your life? Why is it all about you? Why does everybody have to respect you? How about respect for other people? How about respect for your father?"

"Trust me, I have respect for my father."

Bernadette snorted. "You've been having sex with a woman under his roof."

"He doesn't even know about her."

"Maybe when she left crying, with a bag of all her stuff, he got the idea."

Frances shrugged. "Well, she's gone now. So you don't have to worry about anything."

Bernadette let out a long sigh. "You know, I just think you need to put yourself into better situations. Think about your choices." She was using her nice voice now.

"Bernadette, I am not acting on some whim."

"You're twenty years old. You have no idea about anything."

"Ah, Master, you are so wise."

"I'm serious."

"I'm going to bed."

"Frankie, get a grip! Think about somebody besides yourself."

"You first."

Bernadette clasped her hands in front of her chest. "I'm praying for you, Frankie."

Frances was halfway down the stairs. "Don't waste your breath," she called back.

Health

The next day Rita had a dreamy smile on her face. "We're going to make a baby," she confided to Frances. "We can't wait forever. If we wait much longer, we'll be too old. My mother had three children in school by the time she was my age, and another on the way."

Frances nodded. Oscar was in the kitchen with Tomas. The marital bliss had rubbed off on Oscar, who was happily working with his brother, which was just fine with Frances. She had no desire to be in the same room with Tomas.

"You okay, sweetheart?" Rita asked. They were cleaning the last of a small Christmas party from a dentist's office. There had been an impromptu wet T-shirt competition between a totally wasted hygienist and dental assistant. The tables were sticky with beer and cigarette butts.

"What a bunch of idiots."

"Well, those idiots gave us three hundred and fifty dollars. So, today I forgive them."

"My sister is pregnant."

Rita clapped her hands. "Who's the papa?"

France shrugged. "Don't know."

"Well that's fine, too," Rita said. "She's got her sister."

Frances nodded.

"I'm so happy for you. Family is everything. If you have your family and you have your health, you are rich. All this other business –" Rita waved her arm around the empty restaurant "– will pass."

"So they say," Frances said. She grabbed the mop from the bucket and swiped it across the floor. "What a fucking mess."

Collector

At this hour, the suburb was desolate, with no natural distinctive features; flat and sparsely dotted with newly planted trees. Snow whirled across the road in a fury of wind. Settlers had fought drought and blistering cold, recession, depression, boom and bust; they had pretty much decimated the grassland's original human and animal inhabitants only to come up with drab rows of interchangeable raised bungalows occasionally interrupted by strips of low-rent townhouses. Robyn took a long drag on her cigarette; it was kind of funny if you thought about it.

In thirty years, the city will be famous for its sprawl. Robyn will raise a fruit-forward glass of well-structured Syrah to her lips, a line of silver bracelets clattering down her arm. She will pause before sipping and declare to her guests that her vintage aesthetic was born in the foothills, a land populated by cowboys and pumpjacks. That second-hand cowboy boots had launched her career – resources from the west yet again providing income to the east. And she will laugh and her guests will laugh along with her, with Alberta, which, in thirty years' time is what Robyn will be calling herself. She will take on the name as a lark, to upset her mother, but quickly adapt to it – Alberta O, vintage shop proprietor, famous drinker and lover. Alberta O, grown thick across the middle in her fifties but with lavish breasts still bursting forth from her dresses – a cultural influencer with just shy of eight thousand Instagram followers – and fewer than half of those purchased. Her Twitter account was sorrowfully neglected, but who could blame her for staying off Twitter.

But tonight, at this frigid midnight hour, December 1982, she was still known as Robyn. The street, with its puny, skeletal trees, was miserable, even with a fresh coating of snow blanketing the square lawns, even with houses decked out with Christmas lights. Her ripped tights, thrift store cowboy boots and tweed overcoat provided poor protection against a minus-eighteen wind chill. She could not get out of this dump soon enough, but in the meantime, she needed a friendly place to crash. Or something like that. She crushed out her cigarette and marched, swinging her arms military style, across the street.

Robyn dropped her canvas bag, filled with everything she still wanted to own, including her toothbrush, three pairs of black bikini underwear, eyelash curler, black eyeliner and mascara, red lipstick, a copy of *The Electric Kool-Aid Acid Test*, a bag of ripple chips, a pint of vodka, a half-finished deck of Player's Light, a pair of black jeans, a black turtleneck, a balled-up vintage fifties black cocktail dress and a pair of black feather mules pinched from the Salvation Army. Robyn was starting over, if she didn't freeze to death first.

Her plan was to get in as quietly as she could, without waking anyone. The first order of business was to pop the screen from the basement window. The screen came out easily but the window was locked and braced with a sawed-down broomstick. Fuck, she couldn't believe she forgot it was there. It cost her ten bucks to get here by taxi; she couldn't afford to get back downtown. So, Robyn knocked on the small window.

She'd grabbed sixty dollars from the stash Graham kept between the covers of his *Merriam-Webster* dictionary. She deserved it – she deserved more, really – but she didn't want to come off as a bitch, and Graham was saving for a trip to Nashville, or Austin. "I hate country music," she told him, and he said, "It's alt country! Alternative country!" Supposedly he hated country music, too.

Robyn banged more vigorously on the glass. Her fingers were going to fall off, her toes and thighs on fire with cold. She thumped again. Please don't make me have to ring the fucking doorbell. Please don't let Frankie be out somewhere. She hammered repeatedly on the window. Please, not tonight.

A beam of light shone on her face. Robyn covered her eyes and waved.

Frances tugged the window open. "What the hell, Robyn?"

"I have nowhere else to go."

Frances threw her hands up and bugged her eyes.

"I didn't want to wake you," Robyn said.

"That's the stupidest thing I've ever heard you say."

"I'm freezing to death. Literally."

Frances sighed and stepped away from the window. "Come in."

Robyn tossed her bag into the room then wiggled through the window.

"You couldn't have pulled on a pair of jeans?" Frances said.

"I left in the heat of the moment."

"Shocker."

"It's the solstice. Graham was acting all pagany. You know, like we were supposed to think about what we want to release and burn it up in this fire-releasing ceremony, then I lit my smoke with his special candle and he actually accused me of being out of touch with myself." Robyn pulled her cigarettes from her bag. "I'm going to Toronto on Thursday. Mom bought me a ticket. I'm going to stay there a while, you know, hang with Mommy as long as I can stand it. Think about finishing my degree, check out the scene."

"That's sudden," Frances said.

"Not really. She sent me the ticket just after Dad's funeral."

Frances blushed. "You've been planning to go back since September?"

"Maybe. I guess. I hadn't decided if, or for how long." Robyn shrugged. "You know, I didn't want to say anything to you if I wasn't even going to do it. Jesus, it's not much warmer down here."

Frances stomped into her bedroom and returned with her space heater. "I'll get you a sleeping bag," she said.

Robyn was crouched in front of the heater, warming her face and hands when Frances returned. She unrolled the bag and dropped it on the couch. Robyn pulled the heater closer and crawled into the sleeping bag. "Can you throw my coat on top of me?"

Frances tossed the man's overcoat to Robyn. "Good night," she said and closed her bedroom door behind her.

Robyn arranged the coat on top of her sleeping bag. "Why, of course Robyn, I'd love to give you a hand."

On the other side of the door, under her breath, Frances muttered, "Asshole." She climbed back under her covers, pulled her legs into her chest and shivered. She'd been an asshole, too, to believe, even for a minute, that Robyn loved her.

Shortly before her fifty-third birthday, Robyn, now known as Alberta O, was invited to deliver a talk to a small group of business students gathering to share a drink with her, and to hear about O Vintage's move from brick-and-mortar building to web-only store. They hoped also for a chance to speak with her new husband, Stefan Barth, a venture capitalist rumoured to be her driver that evening, networking being key to the universe unfolding in their direction.

Alberta O was splendid. Her breasts spilled forth, as ever, from her low-cut black dress. She sported fishnet stockings and red cowboy boots. Freshwater pearls were slung around her neck, flapper style, and a pair of reading glasses was tucked into her tumbled bun; strands of hair fell haphazard and sexy around her face. Having returned to her natural blonde some years before, Alberta had taken recently to streaking it with violet tones in an effort to downplay the encroachment of grey.

Not that she minded getting old – not very much, anyway. It was better than the alternative, right? Marrying Stefan was a surprising first, but he was a lovely man; a rich art collector with a Muskoka cottage, a spacious downtown high-rise condo and a penchant for warm climate winter holidays. He was a generous lover and not the tiniest bit interested in a conventional bride. Young women, he said, made him grind his teeth. He liked to shake things up, bring his wild wife into rooms filled with conservative business folk. It was a mutually beneficial arrangement. Call that love.

You know what's nice after you turn fifty? Designer made knock-off vintage, that's what's nice. Six-hundred-dollar cowboy boots are especially nice, as are health spas, healing waters and the endless happiness of reaching into your wallet for a twenty and finding one there. And for those days when you've had enough of fishnet stockings and hemlines, a pair of Nudie jeans and a Comme des Garçons T-shirt. So maybe it wasn't such a big surprise that Alberta O found herself courted and wooed and wed at this late point in life. She had always been a pragmatist and Stefan Barth was a positive solution to the problem of aging.

But Alberta O had not been invited to talk about her recent marriage, which, because it was so very conventional, so totally ordinary, caused her a certain amount of embarrassment. No, Alberta O was here to talk about her career. The room was full of budding fashion entrepreneurs, kids really, all staring at her expectantly. She tucked her hair behind her ear and perched herself on the edge of a long table at the front of the room, like a cool teacher would. She swung her legs and smiled.

"The truth is, I stumbled into my work. I have half a bullshit degree in business, entered into for my mother's benefit, but the rest – my life, my work, my training, my *self*-training in business – has been a baptism by fire." Alberta laughed. "Not that I'd have it any other way."

In the spring of 1983, Alberta told the group, she and her mother had flown back to Calgary to take care of some final paperwork regarding her father's estate. Robyn returned to Toronto with four suitcases of cowboy boots purchased from thrift stores and began to sell them out of her dank little basement suite on Salem Avenue. She left out the details of her mother's financing.

Gloria Oliver was, at first, annoyed by her daughter's strange behaviour following her return from Calgary, but eventually she became alarmed. Robyn dug out her old Girl Guides sash and took to wearing it over her appalling skimpy outfits. Robyn, it seemed, wanted to be outlandish for the sake of being outlandish. When Robyn began to insist on being called Alberta her mother tried to send her to a doctor. She wasn't working, she wasn't fit for work, if you asked Gloria, but when she sold those godawful cowboy boots something lit up in her. Gloria was relieved to see her taking up anything resembling a job, although she wore that ridiculous sash for a full year. One day she showed up without the sash and when Gloria asked where it had gone, Robyn replied that her mourning period was over.

"So," she told her audience, "I borrowed my mother's car and started travelling to estate sales anywhere within an easy day's drive. I started building my stash, although I believe the business term would be *inventory*." Smiles and chuckles from her audience. "I suppose I was a little obsessed." She didn't dwell on the fact that the clothes she bought, and the trinkets she dropped covertly into her purse and pockets, belonged to dead people. People buried or burned whose scent lingered on their garments; whose personality showed up in a porcelain figurine, a carved wooden box, a fountain pen or a bowl too small to hold four olives. Twice she'd lifted photographs, probably not for sale, certainly not marked, but what were they doing there anyway? One was a wedding shot of a bride and groom on a wooden porch, squinting into the camera; the other, a mother, hair styled like a flapper's, holding a bald baby on her lap. Dead now, all dead, even the baby, most likely.

She drew a deep breath and launched into her *blah blah*: I couldn't stand sleeping in the back of my store because contrary to popular belief running a vintage shop does not make one rich, guffaw, guffaw, I just wanted to live in an apartment like a regular forty-five-year-old, so I set up a website and moved into a two-bedroom flat and started sourcing vintage reproductions. Oh, and it helps to take some java and html courses so you can do the updates yourself, but don't shirk on web design – remember the mantra: be user friendly. She bored herself with this story.

But they were beautiful, all those young people, listening raptly and scribbling notes, and Alberta was struck with nostalgia. She was overwhelmed with the desire to share something meaningful, something those kids would recognize as true.

"You are young," she said. "So fuck it up. Don't be afraid to lose it all!" She threw her arms in the air. "And fuck everybody. Not over. That shit always comes back to you in business. I mean, make love not war. I mean, your youth is fleeting, please don't tell me the only thing you want to make is money." That was her advice. Anyway, she'd always made more of a reputation than money. "I'll bet you've never heard that at a business meeting."

Some kids laughed. Some kids squirmed and so Alberta told them about her next project, which she'd spontaneously invented as their youth washed over her like a drug. "I've curated a series." My God she loved the word *curated*. "Tchotchkes. Oddities I've gathered over the past twenty-five years or more of rummaging around estate sales and thrift markets." She tucked her hands under her bum; her diamond solitaire dug into her flesh, sharp and comforting. "It'll be a pop-up venture and I'm going to call it Fire Sale. Because for me, that's it, I'm leaving the business. I've decided to retire." Alberta blinked, surprised at her own declaration. "Selling it all."

The students grabbed their phones and began typing furiously and snapping photos. She tilted her chin so her neck wouldn't look wrinkled in the images they were posting (#agelessvintage). There'd be no backing down now, but what the hell, she was bored by everything these days and thinking of becoming a yoga teacher. Or a tea sommelier.

"How about I take some questions," she said.

Arms shot up like flowers in a time-lapse video.

At the gathering after her lecture, Alberta sipped on an acidic glass of red wine entirely lacking in backbone. To be fair, it was a glass of wine she would have happily quaffed before her union with Stefan brought more sophisticated varietals to her palate. A young woman approached Alberta. Her dark hair was cut short and spiky, sections bleached and coloured blue. Jeans hung loosely off her hips. She wore a cropped white T-shirt and black Doc Marten boots.

"Hi," she said.

Alberta, at a loss for words, just smiled and nodded. The girl, the gorgeous young thing, was the image of Frances Murray. Not so much the image of Frankie, but her essence – her shyness, her butchness. Alberta leaned against the wall.

"Would you mind taking a selfie with me?"

Alberta nodded. "Not at all," she said.

The girl tucked herself close to Alberta, snapped a photo and then held it up for Alberta to see.

"My neck looks wrinkled," Alberta said.

"You look great for your age."

"Aren't you sweet," Alberta said. "What's your name?"

"Kim."

"Nice to meet you, Kim."

"My mom buys tons of your stuff. She's going to freak out when I send her this."

Alberta nodded. "Well isn't that thoughtful of you."

Then Kim was gone, off with the other young. Alberta tipped the wine to her lips and finished her glass in a quick swallow. If the rest of the night was going to be taken up with thinking about Frankie she may as well be drunk.

Alberta didn't believe in regrets. She didn't believe in regrets, but she would be a liar if she said she didn't miss Frankie.

However, drinking was an imperfect solution to the problem of relentless nostalgia. Alberta hadn't drunk enough to pass out; she'd had just enough to lay awake and listen to Stefan's even sleep. It occurred to her that Stefan, too, had a bit of Frankie about him, in his easy manner and in his restraint. Stefan was never quick to offer his opinion, although she knew full well he had many.

Eventually Alberta gave up hope of sleeping and carried her laptop to the couch. An Internet search for Frankie brought up what it always did: a link to Frankie's sister Bernadette, who was now a Platinum Club realtor. On Bernadette's homepage there was one small photo, impossible to enlarge, of Bernadette, Mr. Murray, leaning now on a walker, and a young man in his twenties? Thirties? Hard to know. Pumpkins and bales of hay surrounded them. The photo's caption read: *Fall harvest food bank FUNraiser*.

Alberta drifted off on a Frankie fantasy in which she is making Frankie tea – a beautiful, organic, loose-leaf white tea, gently flavoured with jasmine and hibiscus blossoms. In this whimsy they sometimes just hold hands – not because they're going to fuck, Alberta had no intention of being unfaithful to Stefan, but because so much time has passed and there is so much to share, and the ease with which they begin again is so happy-making.

And Frankie tells Alberta she's followed her career and she loves the name change! Frankie tells Alberta she'd always hoped she'd meet her soul sister again.

A flush of embarrassment washed over Alberta. What a crock of shit. Frankie was never going to sit down to tea with her. The closest thing to affection that Frances Murray would have for Alberta O was contempt.

Singer

After she'd finished half the pint of vodka, Robyn tiptoed to Frankie's bedroom and leaned against the door. "Beautiful dreamer, queen of my song, why must you hate me when I've loved you so long?" she crooned. "Beautiful dreamer, awake unto me!" Robyn knocked lightly. "Beautiful dreamer?"

Frances opened her door. "Your little cute routine isn't going to work this time."

Robyn pulled Frances to the couch. "You're my best friend, Frankie."

"That's supposed to make me feel better?"

"I never should have made out with you. I'm sorry, Frankie."

"For fuck's sake, Robyn, it was a little more than just making out."

"I can't be what I'm not."

"What? You can't be kind? You can't be honest?"

"Everything's always so serious with you. You need to learn to have fun."

Frances stood up. "I have shift in a few hours. I'm going back to bed. You can stay here until Thursday, but keep a low profile. My dad won't freak out if he sees you, but he won't be too happy about it. And please, just stay out of my sister's way."

Frances turned back at the door of her bedroom. "We're all up and out early tomorrow morning. You can make some toast and tea while the house is empty. But be out of the kitchen by noon."

"Thanks, Frankie."

Frances shrugged then closed her door.

"You're welcome, Robyn," Robyn whispered.

It wasn't so much that she preferred men to women – though she did. It was just that it was too weird. And other people were weird about it. People got all freaky about that shit. She didn't want to hurt Frankie's feelings. She loved Frankie. She loved Frankie more than anyone, really. But it was just too fucking weird. And Robyn had never said she was a lesbian; that was Frankie's thing. Frankie was being a bit of an asshole, pushing it down her throat the way she was.

Robyn reached for the vodka then remembered she'd grabbed half a joint from the ashtray at Graham's and dropped it in her coat pocket. A little spliff would be the perfect way to end the night. But the effects of the small joint suffused Robyn with energy. She reached for her pint and took a long swallow. What the hell, she may as well go out with a bang, recover tomorrow and fly home all rested and pretty on Thursday.

Robyn heard Frankie in the room, watched through her lashes as Frankie pulled on her jeans, tucked in her white T-shirt and tightened her black belt. Frankie pulled on a navy sweatshirt then stomped up the stairs and out of the basement, not even trying to be quiet. She turned back at the top of the stairs. "Don't go upstairs until my dad and sister have left. I mean it."

"I'm asleep," Robyn said.

"Just don't get me in trouble."

"Why are you waking me up then?"

"I mean it," Frankie said and closed the door behind her.

Robyn stared at the ceiling. She ran her tongue around her dry mouth, a vain effort to ease her thirst. Her head was pounding and she had to go to the bathroom. But that would have to wait or Frankie would have a shit fit. She was going to freeze her tits off down here. Robyn leaned over and cranked the space heater to its maximum, pushed herself back down under the blanket and pulled her overcoat up to her ears. She'd feel better after a couple more hours sleep.

She's drinking water, glass after glass, but is still thirsty. All the water makes her bladder ache. She needs to find a place to piss but the campfire is warm and she doesn't want to lose her spot near the flames. She has to pee so badly and nothing, nothing, will ever quench her thirst.

Warm liquid streamed down her legs and Robyn woke with a start. Her overcoat, what was left of it, had fallen on the space heater. Tall flames were rising from the electric element. The fire had jumped to the wooden coffee table and the heat, after another winter had begun six weeks before winter officially arrived, was soothing. God, she'd peed herself in her sleep! Robyn pulled her tights off and threw them on the coffee table.

She didn't hear any noise from upstairs. Robyn watched her tights melt into the wood. The smoke was thickening and the flames coming off the coffee table were getting close to the ceiling. Robyn climbed over the back of the couch. The cold concrete floor was a shock. She could feel everything: the heat on her face, the freeze against the soles of her feet, the damp urine between her thighs, the smoke creeping into her lungs.

Robyn pushed the couch against the coffee table and headed upstairs. In the kitchen she filled a glass with water and drank it down. She filled it a second time and guzzled. "This is like a crazy dream," she muttered. "This is just a weird dream."

Smoke was creeping through the basement door. Robyn looked at the smoke and screamed, at herself as much as the growing fire coming from the basement. She smacked her palms against her cheeks, three times in rapid succession. She ran through the house to the front door and out onto the street.

History

The streetlight was entirely frozen so that from the top, where the lamp should shine its light, icicles hung. If Jimmy were a poetic man he'd have said it was like a crown of thorns. Firemen, crusted with ice, moved across the yard, and behind them stood Jimmy's house, smoking but no longer blazing. For some reason it made him think of that James Taylor song Bernadette used to sing when she was a teenager. It was so sweet, that innocent girl belting out the lyrics for "Fire and Rain." But then she was never as innocent as all that, not after Barb died. He reached down to his lower left back and pushed his knuckles against the ever-present ache.

The day Jimmy Murray blew out his back for good he was carrying his new bride, Doris (formerly Sister Theresa), across the recently constructed front entry of his first purchased house, a small bi-level on Doverthorn Road. Doris, who had lived twenty-five years on a plain diet, took to variety with gusto. In two short years out of the convent she had learned to cook and enjoy the sensation of being comfortably full, in the process gaining thirty pounds (more to love, if you asked Jimmy). Nevertheless, they both agreed that carrying his new bride across the threshold might have been a rash act for a man approaching fifty and a bride approaching 170 pounds.

Jimmy stumbled and let Doris slip. He grabbed the wall with one hand and his back with the other. "Judas Priest!"

"I told you it was a bad idea," Doris said. By then she'd managed to get Jimmy into bed and tucked a heating pad just above his left hip.

"I'd do it again." Jimmy pulled Doris down on top of him. "We got a couple of hours until Frankie gets home," he said. "Be gentle with me."

Doris smiled, stood up and slipped out of her dress and underwear, and carefully climbed on top of her husband.

Doris had been the answer that turned Jimmy into a praying man. Hell if he could explain what she saw in him. But when Jimmy was kissing Doris, he turned into a better version of himself. He was Bogart and she was Bacall, or Tracy and Hepburn. But things went to shit faster than you could say things went to shit and Doris died at lightning speed.

Jimmy knew of people who responded to treatment, who rallied, who lingered, who mysteriously healed because of their strong will or good luck. But whatever it was that saved those folks, Jimmy and Doris were in short supply. Not that Doris complained; in fact, she'd say downright stupid things like, "Cancer is a word not a sentence," and Jimmy would agree because there would be no point to telling a dying woman you never heard her say such a stupid thing. What would be the point in that?

So Doris did a round of chemo that left her scorched, hairless and skin hanging. Thank God she weighed 170 going in, though the picture of Doris decimated by her treatment and lying on the couch, watching the tearful funeral of Terry Fox while the sun blazed through the front window, was never going to leave Jimmy.

And she had the gall that afternoon to say, "Now that's a tragedy," because, even if the chemo wasn't taking, she'd had twice the time that poor kid had been given. Jimmy kept his mouth shut, bit his tongue, but didn't they deserve another twenty, thirty years themselves? Apparently not because the cancer just moved on in military fashion, marching through her insides, laying waste.

When Doris was gone – suddenly it felt like, despite all the months of her fading away – there was an awful silence. If Doris had been able to speak, she would have called her death the end of an era, like when Frankie flew off to gallivant around Europe and Jimmy, liberated of daughters, pushed Doris against the kitchen counter and reached under her blouse, and she laughed and said, "Here's to the start of a new era."

Jimmy snorted, because there it was, all that was left of his house – the bones – and he wasn't even seeing it; he was letting his thoughts go to Doris, and why not? What was the point in looking now? Jimmy stomped his feet and shivered. Well, at least he wasn't going to have to worry about making the mortgage any more. He looked to the truck where Bernadette sat perched behind the steering wheel, chewing gum and blowing bubbles. Furious. He could see that much. Frankie sat behind her, looking at him, but Jimmy couldn't find a smile for her. He'd been happy (happy being a relative term; glad might be a better way to say it) to see her come back, but now – well, all he knew was, whatever he had left of Doris was ash and covered in ice inside the smoking frame of his dream home, if that's what you called it – that's what Doris called it – and Frankie had a hand in it. She'd brought that girl in and he couldn't even begin to think about what else they'd gotten up to under his roof. But this was what it had come to; he couldn't shake the feeling that Frances, and maybe him, too, by overlooking what was right in front of his eyes, had brought retribution down upon them all.

Fire Brigade

"Look what you started," Bernadette hissed.

"Me?" Frances said.

"You let her in."

"Because she would have frozen to death if I hadn't. Literally frozen to death."

"I wish she had."

"Jesus, Bernie."

Bernadette shrugged. "What do you want me to say? That's it's totally excellent to find out my sister is a deviant and that her stupid little fuck of a friend burned our house down, and that's super great because now it's three days before Christmas and Santa is going to bring us a new house, all because my stupid dyke of a sister let a fucking psycho into our house, yippee?"

Frances drew in a sharp breath. "Holy shit, Bern," she whispered. "You just crossed a line, man ..."

"I'm sick as a dog and have nowhere to lie down. Do not lecture me about crossing lines when you've crossed them all yourself. You should have known better. You shouldn't have been so selfish."

"Selfish?"

"How do you think Dad and I feel with you flaunting yourself all over the place? Like you're special or something. Here's a little insight: you're not special."

"I didn't flaunt anything!"

Bernadette snorted.

"You burst into my room!"

"Under Dad's roof, Frankie. How trashy can you get?"

"Said the woman who doesn't know where the guy who knocked her up went to."

"What I did was natural."

"Fucking a stranger is natural?"

"Fucking a man is natural."

"How about I go ask Dad. You know, what he thinks about your natural behaviour." Frances pushed open the door of the truck and jumped out.

"You wouldn't dare!"

"Hey, Dad!" Frances called.

Jimmy turned toward Frances and watched as Bernadette bolted out of the driver's seat and tackled her sister. Frances fell forward, her face banging hard into the frozen ground. His girls lay there breathing heavily, hugging one another it seemed, until Frances lifted her head. Blood flowing from her nose. She roared, shook her sister off her back, pushed herself to her knees and slapped Bernadette across the head. She raised her hand for another blow when Jimmy stepped between them.

"What the hell is going on?"

Frances wiped the blood off her face with her mitts. "Bernadette has some news for you, Dad."

"Yeah, Frankie's going to hell," Bernadette said. "With the rest of her kind."

"That's right, me and all the pregnant teenagers." Frankie clapped her hands. "Oh, wait! Bernie, you're not a teenager this time!"

"What?" Jimmy said.

"I'm going to start calling you Gramps!" Frances said.

"Stop it!" Jimmy said.

"You all right here?" a fireman asked.

"Just burning off some steam," Jimmy answered.

The fireman nodded and walked away.

"You two ought to be ashamed," Jimmy said.

Frances shrugged.

Jimmy looked at Bernadette. "Is she saying you're pregnant?"

Bernadette nodded.

"Well," he said, "a baby coming is a little bit of good news. You going to bring the father around this time?"

She shook her head.

Jimmy rubbed his lip. Nodded. "I guess we're just going to have to make that work then."

"What about me?" Frances asked.

"What about you?" Jimmy said. "I can't believe you hit your sister when you knew she was pregnant."

"What?"

"If you want so much to be like a man, then act like a man."

"I've never said I want to be a man."

"You could have fooled me," Jimmy said.

"I should be able to count on you two," Frances said.

"Would you be counting on us if you robbed a bank, too?" Bernadette asked.

Frances shook her head. "I can't believe you made that comparison. But actually, yes, I would."

It crossed Jimmy's mind then that it might actually be easier to tell people Frankie was a robber.

"You want us to tell you it's okay," Bernadette said. "But it's not. It's sinful and it's just not something you brag about. And it's sickening to think of you like that."

Frances looked at Jimmy. "You don't really believe that?"

But Jimmy said nothing. He stuffed his hands into his coat pockets and pursed his lips. Then he turned away and looked back at the smouldering house.

Frances nodded, tears – horrifyingly – rolled down her cheeks. She threw her bloodied mitts on the ground, stuffed her hands in her pockets and walked away.

Tenderfoot

Robyn leaned her head against the window of the jet as it lifted into the air and the city dropped away. In its place, a wide expanse of farmland draped in snow thin enough that she could see the shape of the quarter sections, white square beside white square. She should remember this, the bird's-eye view of farm fields in winter. She should think of this and not of yesterday, when she ran across the street and the lady there opened the door and there were four kids eating apple slices and watching *Sesame Street*, and they looked at her like she was a maniac. The lady said, "Oh my God," and Robyn turned with her to look at the flames that reached out of the basement window and up the front of the house.

And she shouldn't think of Frankie, who rushed back to the scene with her father and sister, refusing to listen to her, refusing to get out of her dad's truck. And she shouldn't think of Mr. Murray waving her off, saying, "Just go now, Robyn, just go. The damage is done."

Robyn took a deep, calming breath. The emergency room doctor had sent her off with a half dozen little white Xanax pills to cope with the shock. Robyn popped the last two tranquilizers in her mouth and waited for the images of Big Bird on the TV screen, of the flames jumping up the outside walls of the house, of Frankie unyielding in her dad's truck, and of Mr. Murray flapping his arms and sending her away to quiet down. To just quiet the fuck down.

Globetrotter

Frances lifted the shade that covered the window; the sun, mostly obscured by cloud, was rising in the east over Europe. It was impossible to see the Atlantic below. She pulled the shade back down and closed her eyes.

The worst week of her life, bar none, *ha ha.*

Tomas met her at Tim Horton's with a thousand bucks in hand. A call to the Lesbian Information Line got her hooked up with a free place to crash while she sorted out her passport, which happily was intact but smelled like a bonfire – a little memento of the destruction. Whatever, it got her the fuck out of Calgary. It would get her back to London, and she was sure she would find Reena once she made her way to Greenham. Someone at the camp would know who Reena was and where to find her.

She should have asked Tomas for two grand – he was scared shitless of her. Scared shitless she would tell Rita what she'd seen, as if Rita didn't already have her suspicions. And if she could have said something without hurting Rita, she would have gone for it, but what the fuck, he was broke anyway. Like her dad, like Bernadette, like the whole city.

She thought they might look for her, her dad and Bernie, but not a word and, as usual, she was an idiot to hope for more. Fuck them. If they thought she was going to come crawling back they were idiots, too, which they were. They were fucking assholes.

Her chest, her shoulders, her legs ached. But she would go to Reena and sleep it off; surely she would be able to sleep once she was there. And even if Reena hated her, Frances was pretty sure she would help her and then she could figure out what was next.

May 2016

You & Others

Phoenix tucked the quilt in around his grandfather's shoulders. The brightly coloured disappearing nine-patch design had been his grandpa's favourite these past few years. It was a simple technique, Jimmy said, but if a guy used his colours just right he could make it look real hard.

The old man opened his eyes. "Frankie?"

"It's Phoenix, Grandpa."

"Brandon?"

"Yes."

"You're not Frankie."

Phoenix nodded and took his grandfather's hand.

"Frankie." Jimmy's eyes welled with tears. "I thought you weren't coming."

"I'm here."

Bernadette sat on a green brocade loveseat across from Jimmy's bed. Ostensibly she was reading through listings and ignoring the two men. Still, it rankled, her dad's desire to see Frankie, as though she wasn't the one who walked away, as though she wasn't the one who couldn't be bothered. It was no secret where she and Jimmy were; they hadn't just walked off into the proverbial sunset. But even though she'd stuck around and kept a roof over her dad's head, he gave her no credit at all.

Later, after Jimmy had fallen asleep and she and Phoenix were at Earls for a quick supper before returning to the hospice, she asked, "Do you think you're being wise?"

"What do you mean?" Phoenix said.

"Leading him on. Letting him think you're Frankie."

"A lie told for the greater good is pretty much the same thing as telling the truth."

Bernadette rolled her eyes.

Phoenix shrugged. "If it makes him happy it doesn't bother me."

"He's going to think you've never come to him."

"So?"

"So when he says where was Brandon –"

"Phoenix."

"I'm serious."

"I am too."

Bernadette sighed heavily. "You think you understand, but you don't know the half of it."

"Actually, I think I have a pretty good idea." He took a long drink of his beer then set the pint back down. "I know you guys blamed her because she's queer."

"I did not!"

"I've talked to Grandpa, you know."

Bernadette shook her head. "Where is all this hostility coming from?"

"I can't believe you guys never even looked for her." Phoenix slapped his chest. "I feel that."

Bernadette opened her mouth then closed it again. She didn't want to fight with Brandon. "My dad is dying. Can't you just cut me some slack?"

"I just think that it could have just as easily been me."

"No. It couldn't have been you. No. Not even for a second. Anyway, times have changed. I'm fine with it."

Phoenix raised his eyebrows but said nothing.

"She did some terrible things, too, you know," Bernadette said.

"You could have found her. You could have told her about Grandpa."

"Do you know what, Brandon –"

"Phoenix," he snapped.

"Well, you know what, Phoenix? She was found. I sent her three letters. All of them came back unopened with *return to sender* written on them. Dad even found one of them. So imagine how I felt."

"I'm too busy imagining how she felt."

"Like I said," Bernadette snapped, "you don't know the half of it." She opened her bag and threw a twenty on the table. "There's some cab fare. I'll pay for the bill on my way out. See you back at the hospice, I have to make some calls first."

"Whatever," Phoenix said.

"Don't get on your high horse," she said.

Through the window, Phoenix watched his mother stomp to her car while she punched numbers into her phone. He'd meant to keep quiet. What was the point of stirring it all up now? But staying silent was a betrayal of something. Maybe he wasn't betraying an aunt he wouldn't know if he passed her on the street, but to not call his mom on her shit was just wrong. If she believed her sister was so bad, then it followed that she believed the same of him, even if she said otherwise.

He watched as Bernadette climbed into her Lincoln; she was all business now. Making deals on her BlackBerry. He eyed the twenty she'd left on the table; he didn't need her money, but she still liked to throw it around. He would give it back to her, but then she'd accuse him of being petulant and act offended, and Grandpa would be stressed by the discord and cry, or something worse. So Phoenix tucked the twenty under his beer glass. At least he could make the waitress happy.

Domestic Service

There was no point in staying any longer at that table with Brandon.

He was so quick to judge, but she *did* try to remember that he wanted to be called Phoenix, even though it was embarrassing. Because that's what he wanted, *because Phoenix was the name that best reflected his nature,* she was trying. Did she love it? Not one bit. Not one bit, but she was trying.

Father Joe counselled her that each and every person is a sinner in need of God's grace, so who was she to presume that one cross was greater than another? She was to pull him closer and she was to pray for him and she was to sacrifice for him. Which is exactly why she'd left the table without really giving Brandon a piece of her mind. And it's why she called him by his stupid name, too.

Because she was doing her best. And she had been unfailingly polite to her son's boyfriends even though time had proved again and again that none of them were right for Brandon. (Bernadette four, homophobia zero.)

She had worked hard for this family, and she'd been happy to do it. Her kid even studied theatre design, of all things, and got out of school without a penny of debt because she had busted her chops so he could follow his so-called dream. And it was a credit to her that he was making a living decorating sets on all the cowboy shows they liked to shoot out here. Oh, he was doing just fine. He'd found his people.

And Bernadette knew that Brandon thought her faith was irrational, but what was she without her faith? What was anybody? She would have been nothing. A lonely single mother picking up strangers or, worse yet, married to some bastard who kept her under his foot. But the church, and Jesus, with a little help from Saint Jude (her people!) raised her up and she had accomplished the impossible. She had brought herself and her father and son from literally nothing to where they were now, which was a damn sight better than half the people on this planet.

So whatever. Brandon could judge her all he wished, but she would keep praying for her beautiful little boy, for whom she was eternally grateful even when she wanted to throttle him. And there was that other little baby, who it still stung to think of, though some days it was impossible not to. Forty-one now, presumably happy. Certainly not curious about her, and that was a blessing, too – that he was happy enough in his life to have no curiosity about hers. How could she see that as anything but a blessing? It was a blessing.

Bernadette turned down the hall toward Jimmy's room and pushed open the door. "Hey, Dad," she said. "I brought you a Popsicle."

Jimmy smiled brightly. "Hey there, good looking." But when she tried to pass him the Popsicle his eyes went vacant and he turned his head away, his lips moving through a quiet litany of which she could make no sense.

"I'll get the nurses to put it in the freezer for later," Bernadette said, but it was already melting so she dropped it in the garbage.

She stood at the end of his bed and rubbed his feet through the blankets. His hair stood on end like he'd been electrocuted. Her big, old dad, so thin now and fragile; melting away just like the orange Popsicle.

Bernadette brushed a tear from her cheek.

She never would have guessed she would miss him this much.

September 2015

Traveller

Frances and Reena sat in silence while the taxi raced along the Deerfoot heading into Calgary.

"Have you missed it?" Reena asked.

Frances shook her head.

"It's all very new here."

"Yes," Frances said.

They weren't expected until the next morning and so they had some time to defrag in their hotel room. Frances was on the bed. Reena lay down beside her.

"I think I'm having a heart attack."

Reena pulled Frances close. "You aren't."

"We shouldn't have come."

"We had to come."

"Well, it's a total mindfuck."

Reena kissed her cheek and stood up. "I'll pour us a little whiskey. Let's just keep a low level in the blood for the rest of the day. And maybe you'll sleep."

"Maybe," Frances said. "But I doubt it."

"But it's worth a try."

"I may as well be drunk."

"We're just going to take the edge off, darling."

"I'll do my best." Frances took a glass from Reena, swirled the amber liquid then raised it to her lips.

"Whoa," Frances said as the cab parked in front of a large infill house. The modern home was sleek and tall, its exterior made up of slate tile, wood and windows. A large steel-and-glass door allowed for easy views of an open staircase flanked by a slate wall that ran the height of the building, as seen through the second-floor windows.

"Fancy," Reena murmured.

The front door opened and Jimmy stepped out, braced by a walker. He was smaller than Frances remembered. His pants were belted tight around his waist but baggy through the hips and legs; the hunch of his back, his chest curling inward, his hair white but still slicked with Brylcreem. Her dad was an old man. Frances and Reena stepped out of the taxi and walked toward Jimmy.

"Aren't you a sight for sore eyes," Jimmy said. "Aren't you a beautiful girl?" When Frances reached him, he pulled her close into a hug and said, "Aren't you an angel?"

"If by angel you mean fat and middle-aged," Frances said.

Jimmy laughed. "Come inside. I made coffee, but we've got to drink it in the kitchen. All the white in this living room is just begging for disaster. I tell you, I'm getting sloppier every day. My hands just conk out on me. Cream? Sugar?"

"Let me," Frances said. "You sit down."

"Well, the cream's in the fridge and the sugar's on the shelf up there." Jimmy pointed. He breathed deeply. "Just look at you, kiddo."

Frances smiled at him.

"And look at you," Jimmy said to Reena. He took her in then. Her long black hair was striped with grey and hung in a neat braid down her back. She wore jeans, a T-shirt and black ankle boots. A small, gold nose stud and large man's watch were her only pieces of jewelry. Her smooth, brown face was handsomer than in the photo that Frances had emailed him. "You're awfully pretty," he said to Reena. Then to Frances he said, "You did well."

Frances passed Reena a mug and carried the other two to the table. "I did," she said. "I was lucky."

Reena smiled.

"I can see that," Jimmy said. "I can sure see that."

Silence fell over the table. Jimmy blew on his coffee.

"Thank you for coming, Frankie. I know I don't deserve it."

"Who's to say who deserves anything, Dad?"

"I wish I hadn't let you go."

"Yeah?"

"It took me time. But yeah."

Frances nodded.

"Your nephew there, Phoenix. He's as gay as they come."

Frances laughed.

"Once I realized, I thought it was pretty funny, too."

"I'm sorry. I'm a little nervous."

"I figured God meant for me to figure something out, but by then ten years had passed, and even if I knew how to find you, I thought it better to leave good enough alone. I didn't want to upset your sister." He sighed. "She's been good to me."

"I can see," Frances said.

"But some nights I'd start thinking about all the bad that could have happened to you –"

"Dad," Frances cut him off, "things worked out for me. And, I dare say, much for the better than if I'd stayed here. I don't want to talk about what you should have done. Or what Bernie should have done. Or what I should have done. It will just make us feel shitty. And this is weird enough."

"I shouldn't have asked you to come."

"I'm glad you did."

Tears slipped out of Jimmy's eyes. "What a goddamn waste."

"Yes."

"I don't know how I let it slide by." Jimmy was crying in earnest now.

"It's okay," Frances lied.

"Bernie means well, but she's a hard nut. I made mistakes with her, too."

"How is this helping? I don't see how this helps."

"Jimmy," Reena said gently. "Do you think we might see your quilts? We'd love to see your work."

Jimmy wiped his nose with the back of his hand and nodded. He pushed himself up. "I'm all set up just off the kitchen here. I've only got a few left. I haven't had the heart this past year or more for nothing big. I've been knitting toques for the winter. And Bernie got me *The Rockford Files* on disc, so I'm happy, as long as I don't think too much."

Jimmy's quilts were a revelation. Abstract and geometric. Squares brightly floating in the middle of a blanket. Whatever constrained him in his daily life was let loose in the designs he built. And the wave of remorse that had just run through him now tore through Frances, an anxious twist of shame and then outrage. That they'd let her go, that they'd believed she was tainted or whatever the fuck.

"You all right?" Reena asked.

Frances shook her head.

Jimmy pulled out a quilt, a riot of gold and green and blue. "This is my favourite. I made it with Doris in mind, with the feel of losing her. And you, too, Frankie. I want you to take it."

"What about Bernie?"

Jimmy shrugged. "She's not here to object. I've written a will. She'll read it."

"You don't think she'll be upset? Us coming behind her back?"

"Well now, I don't think I could have taken any fighting from you two." He sat down. "I just wanted to see you once more. To tell you I'm sorry. She's been awfully good to me, but, like I said, she's a hard nut and I'm just this far from being dead. It's better she's on her trip. Things have been going to shit in this town again and she's worried about money, though for no good reason. She's doing fine, but she likes to fret. Anyway, the desert makes her feel good. I suppose it's childish to sneak around, but seeing you now." He took a deep breath. "I don't think you'd like her now any more than you did then."

"What does that mean?"

"Oh, she'd be all worked up over your mannish look. She's a classy dresser. She likes her fancy shoes."

Reena bit back a laugh.

"You know, Dad, it's probably better if you just stop trying to explain things. Bernie's not here and I can live with that. I can totally live with that."

"She's good with Phoenix."

"Thanks for the quilt, Dad."

"But you two are like oil and water."

"Why don't we go out for lunch?" Reena said.

"I know, Dad. Honestly, I don't need confirmation from you."

"Frannie, we've only got twenty-four hours," Reena said. "Let's take your dad out."

Jimmy was crying again.

"I'm going to need another year's therapy after this trip," Frances whispered.

"Maybe you'd like some lunch, Jimmy?" Reena said.

"I could stand a cold beer."

Reena took his arm. "I think we all could."

After lunch and drinks, Jimmy napped on his recliner and Frances sprawled on the leather couch, snoring lightly. Dr. Oz, on the TV, nattered on in the background. Reena made her way upstairs, compelled, despite herself, to understand these strangers that Frannie was related to. Or just to snoop, whatever. Frances and Jimmy were sleeping, what else was she to do? She couldn't abide Dr. Oz.

The house was styled mid-century modern. The common area, which could just as easily have been a family room, was furnished with a desk and white leather chairs, like a posh solicitor's office. There was a framed photo on the desk, Jimmy and (presumably) Bernadette and Phoenix standing amid pumpkins and bales of hay, all smiling happily. Bernadette was dressed in jeans, heeled boots and a bulky cowl-neck sweater – very Sue Ellen Ewing or some other rich American housewife. (Never married but nevertheless rich, Reena had to give her that.) Jimmy was zipped into a father-knows-best sweater and the young man, Phoenix, wore skinny jeans turned up to expose high-top trainers, a checkered shirt and corduroy jacket, hair pulled back into a short ponytail. Reena liked him already.

The art on the walls was generic and forgettable – surprising given the obvious quality and cost of the furniture. Why there wasn't at least a quilt hanging on the wall was beyond her. Bernadette's bedroom was more of the same: neat, mid-century and generic. White walls, white bedding. There were, however, two standout pieces on the bedroom walls: Above Bernadette's bed was a large, framed black-and-white photograph of a lone pumpjack on a wheat-covered field below a stormy sky. Moody. And affixed above the bedroom door was a large, baroque crucifix. It was both creepy and smashing. It said something about Bernadette. Reena wasn't sure what, but her curiosity was piqued.

Bernadette had her own full-size bathroom attached to her room. A square rain shower head, nice touch. A double guest bed occupied the smallest upstairs room, and a library was housed in the third room. The library was another strange mix: a rack of books on popes and the Catholic faith, plus shelves full of paperback romance novels. Based on the books' cover art, Bernadette had a penchant for cowboys. Well, why not? Reena herself always liked the idea of the child Frances as a cowboy-girl running around the grasslands.

Reena had been tired and filthy when Frances found her in Greenham. She was bundled in her sleeping bag under a tarp attached to a tree, recovering from another anxious, wakeful night waiting to be dragged out from under her makeshift tent. It was six weeks from her arrival at the camp and ten days since the Embrace the Base protest. The exhilaration had worn off. Reena wanted a bath and a bed. And she hated herself for wanting a bath and a bed. The camp was so important, so urgent and all she could focus on was feeling cold and lonely.

"Reena?"

A surge of adrenaline flushed Reena's face. She sat up in her sleeping bag and stared at Frances.

"I'm sorry to just show up on you."

"You look like shit," Reena said.

"I thumbed a ride."

"Christmas holiday?" Reena asked.

Frances shook her head. She started to cry.

"Oh Jesus, Frannie." Reena stood up. "You're the last person I expected to see. I don't know what you want. And I don't know why you're here."

"I didn't have anywhere else to go."

"Really, Frannie? You had absolutely nowhere else to go?"

Frances shrugged. "I wanted to see you."

"Well you're looking at me," Reena said sharply.

In the end, Reena took Frances back to her parents' house. Her mother gave Frances her brother's room. Frances soon found work in the kitchen of the Red Fox pub and moved into a place above the tavern. Reena began training in a sign shop, in her spare time designing posters for women's dances and political actions and concerts. On her days off, Frances joined Reena and her parents for tea. Their days took on a rhythm.

It was nearly a year before Reena kissed Frances.

Frances said, "I was afraid you were never going to do that again."

"I suppose you're not so bad after all," Reena said.

Thirty-two years later, Reena found herself across the ocean, standing in a room in Calgary and trying to get a sense of Frannie's people. As Reena shook off her reverie, the green-lettered spine of a book caught her eye. She pulled out *The Guide Handbook* and turned it over in her hands. The front cover was scorched, but the book had survived that old fire. And Bernadette had kept it, which was something. Perhaps she should take it down to Fran – but why then? To stir up more bad feelings? If she came up and found it, well obviously it was meant to be, but otherwise Reena couldn't see the point of very possibly making things any worse for Frannie than they already were.

Back in the TV room, Frances was staring quietly at the ceiling. "Find anything?" she asked.

"Your sister is quite the Catholic," Reena said.

"Surprise, surprise."

Reena tucked herself in beside Frances. "Are you managing fine?"

"Yes. Aside from feeling like an alien."

"Any regrets?"

Frances shook her head. "What would be the point?"

"Not everything has to have a point, Fran."

Frances closed her eyes. "I don't believe in regret."

Jimmy wept again the next morning as he saw them off.

"Dad –"

"I can't help it." He placed his hand on Frances's cheek. "You are perfect as you are," he said. "I wish I'd told you sooner."

"Say the word and I'll come right back."

Jimmy waved his hand. "All that cost. I've got you here now," he tapped his head. "And here, too." He placed his hand on his heart. "I've got everything I need. I won't ask for more."

Frances kissed Jimmy. She hoped like hell she had what she needed.

"You two take care of each other," Jimmy said.

Reena hugged him. "Goodbye, Jimmy."

"Goodbye, Dad."

Frances didn't look back as the taxi pulled away from the curb.

"What if we run into your sister in Palm Springs?"

Frances shrugged. "We can just stay in tonight. They're gone tomorrow."

"Ships passing in the night."

"So it seems."

June 2016

Hostess

Frances found Reena in the back garden hanging freshly laundered bed linens from the guest rooms. New B&B visitors would be arriving in two hours. Frances had finished preparing a charcuterie platter and a separate fruit and cheese board. She'd brought up the wine, done as much as she could to get ready for breakfast tomorrow and then checked the post. Now, mercifully, they had the house to themselves. She passed a small envelope to Reena then sat on the iron bench.

"What's this?"

"Read it."

Reena pulled a funeral card out of the envelope then unfolded a small letter. She read it quickly and then sat beside Frances and took her hand.

"I'm sorry," she said.

Frances shrugged. "I lost him a long time ago."

"But your nephew!"

"What do you think?"

"Of course he should come. I'd love to meet him."

They sat in silence. The cotton sheets fluttered on the line.

"The rooms are ready?" Frances asked.

Reena nodded. "It's times like this I wish I still smoked."

"I guess I'll invite him to come stay."

"Brilliant."

"You think so?"

Reena nodded. "I do."

"Done then," Frances said.

"Perhaps you'd also like to invite Bernadette?"

"You can't be serious."

"Could it be any more awkward than the visit with your father?"

"Spoken like someone who's never met my sister."

"In for a penny, in for a pound, I say."

"Well, if you're looking for a way to slow down time, inviting my sister is a pretty good plan."

Reena laughed.

"Oh, why the fuck not?" Frances said. She let her head drop onto Reena's shoulder.

Reena pulled Frances close.

In the garden next door, starlings began to chatter loudly. Frances let the birdsong wash over her. She thought of her father and what they'd lost, what they'd never had. There was no point in fighting the tears.

July 1974

Neighbourhood

Bernadette stood on the wooden porch. She stared across the trailer park and trimmed her fingernails with her teeth. Frankie had taken off again, but it was Bernadette who would catch hell when their dad came home. The little brat took off whenever she wanted. It wasn't fair.

Bernie spat out the trimmings, turned on her heel and stomped back inside the trailer. She grabbed her Player's off the counter, turned on the TV and flopped onto the couch. She placed a cigarette between her lips and, as she lit it, a wave of nausea surged. Bernadette closed her eyes against her blossoming understanding and inhaled deeply.

Naturalist

Frankie pulled a string of hair from her mouth. From where she lay on the ground, the cloud that blew across the sky looked like the trail from one of Bern's smokes. She kicked her legs against the thought of her sister, rubbed her left palm against her gun's holster. Bern was as ornery as they come, as usual. She woke up on the wrong side of the bed, that's what their mom would have said. Maybe Mom was watching from heaven now, and she saw how mean Bernie was, and someday she was going to punish Bern with some plague from above that covered her face in zits or made her front tooth fall out so that she would look like a hobo. Frankie would laugh her guts out. And Bernadette would cry.

But later she would help Bern. She would carve her a tooth from stone or find a cure for zits. Or she would pray so hard that Mom would talk to God and He would forgive Bern and make her pretty again, and then He would let Frankie be invisible just for being nice to Bern. She wouldn't use her invisibility to harm people; she would only use it for observation. Well, maybe she would use her invisibility against Bern, but only in self-defence.

Her stomach grumbled with hunger. Frankie had taken off without food while Bern was in the bathroom putting on makeup, and she wasn't going back until suppertime. So what if she got grounded? Bern would get in trouble, too, especially if Frankie cried a little.

She pulled up a long spear of wheat grass and popped its white root into her mouth. She rolled onto her stomach and let her cheek press against the grass and dirt. She should listen for horses, but there were no horses here anymore. There were no trains here and no bank robbers. Just grass, a few crappy trees and a shit-ton of ground squirrels.

Outdoors in the City

Frankie opened her eyes with a start – there was a bug crawling on her cheek. She brushed it from her face and rolled onto her back to find a near perfect girl standing above her. The girl's blonde hair was tied into two neat braids down the length of her back. Instead of cut-offs she wore pressed pink shorts, a pink and white striped T-shirt and navy blue canvas sneakers.

"I thought you were dead," the girl said.

"Maybe I am," Frankie said.

"How can you talk if you're dead?"

"If you were an angel."

"I guess so."

Frankie sat up, pulled her rubber thongs from her back pockets and slipped them onto her feet.

The girl crouched down beside Frankie but didn't let her bum touch the grass. "You seemed dead."

"I was camouflaged."

"What's your name?" the girl asked.

"Frances," Frankie said. "But you can call me Frankie."

"I'm Robyn, because on April tenth my mom heard a robin when she woke up and thought spring was here and then she went into labour. She thought it would never end, but I was finally born on April eleventh and my mom decided to not go through that again, not even for a son. But, anyway, my dad had a son before he got divorced from his first wife."

Frankie had never met anyone who was divorced, but the girl didn't look that bad. "I'm Frances, because of the saint."

"Why were you camouflaged?"

"I'm tracking some gophers."

"That explains it," Robyn said.

"Explains what?"

"You're kind of dirty, if you haven't noticed."

Frankie's cheeks burned.

"Doesn't your mom get mad?" Robyn asked.

"No."

"Lucky you."

"I guess."

"Where do you live?"

"Amylorne Mobile Home Park," Frankie said. "Where do you live?"

"In Bonavista. My mom got mad and said she'd rather have a GD man-made lake than nothing so my dad got us a house at the lake," Robyn said. "Do you like swimming?"

"I guess."

"Maybe one day I'll take you swimming. If your mom says yes."

Frankie's stomach growled. "I should go home for lunch."

"Lunch was a long time ago."

Frankie squinted into the sun. "My mom might be mad," she said.

"Do you want to play tomorrow?" Robyn asked.

"I don't know." The girl asked a lot of questions.

"I'll bring a picnic."

"Maybe, if I can."

"I'll meet you here at ten thirty," Robyn said.

Frankie turned toward the hum of traffic along Macleod, where a strip mall and car dealership were germinating, readying to sprout. "If I can," she repeated.

Robyn waved enthusiastically. "I'll be waiting!"

Frankie licked her finger then lifted it to test the direction of the wind. The other side of Macleod was to the west so she was walking south. A breeze blew across her finger, but she couldn't tell from where. The girl didn't know that though. Frankie slowed her pace. Bernadette would kick her ass if she went in now, but Bern was too stupid to look in the shed, and if Frankie was really quiet she might hear her sister on the phone. And, if she were really lucky, Frankie would hear something she could use against Bernie later, because, like her dad said, Bern was a bloody loose cannon.

Emergency Helper

Jimmy Murray would be the first to tell you he was born to be happy. Jesus Murphy, who wasn't? But some days, happiness needed a little nudge. He poured three fingers of rum into a glass, topped it with Coke and a single ice cube. Bernadette had stormed out of the house in a snit and now Frankie was sulking on the top bunk.

There was never any guessing what would send one off, and getting the other to talk was like squeezing water from a rock. Problem was they were all missing Barb's touch. Barb, who had just stepped out for milk and a deck of smokes when some old fucker mistook his gas pedal for the brake and smashed so hard into the back of a Pinto that it gained the curb and sent Barb flying into the middle of the road. The cops came to find Jimmy in the shop. He followed their car in his truck, off to Holy Cross to identify his dead bride, one of the constables riding beside him to keep him calm during the drive. It may be that God worked in mysterious ways but Jimmy didn't see a bloody mystery in such a loss, just meanness.

Jimmy held his drink carefully aloft and flopped onto the couch. Christ almighty, his back was killing him.

"Dad?" Frankie stepped out of her room and leaned against the kitchen counter.

Jimmy raised his eyebrows in response.

"How come Bern gets to go out?"

"That's the million-dollar question, darling."

"Because it's not fair."

"Well, first off, Bernadette is sixteen. That means she gets to do what you don't."

"But you said she was grounded."

"Frankie, reining Bernadette in is a little bit like tying down the wind."

"What?"

"It's not easy for Bernadette, losing her mother just as she became a teenager."

Frankie blinked back tears and nodded. She chewed on the end of her thumb.

"Her friends are free to run around all summer and she has to stay home with you."

"I can take care of myself."

Jimmy eyed Frankie: her feet and legs were streaked with dirt; her brown hair, which was cropped in a straight line across her chin, was badly in need of a brush. She was half animal. But her hips had recently struck out on their own and now her cut-offs were stretched so tight that the fly cover pulled away from the zipper. Tiny new breasts poked against her T-shirt. Damned if he wouldn't have to send the girls to Woodward's before school began so Bernadette could get her sister a bra.

"Well, darling," Jimmy said, "you're not quite twelve, are you? But next summer you can be entirely on your own if you like."

"I could do it now."

"I'm not interested in arguing. Go have a bath and brush your hair."

"How come I'm grounded and Bernadette's not?"

"Did you hear what I said?"

"It's not like she does anything."

"Frances Mary Murray!"

Frankie spun on her heel. "I'm going," she said and stomped into the bathroom.

Jimmy tipped his glass to his mouth, opened his throat and swallowed the rest of his drink. He spit the ice cube back into the glass, wiped his mouth and stepped up to the counter to mix another drink.

Keep Fit

Frankie lay in bed listening to her father's truck sputter to life and then drive on out of earshot. Seven fifteen – Bern would be asleep for at least three more hours. She padded quietly to the kitchen, grabbed a box of Cap'n Crunch from the cupboard and poured it into a bowl. She'd heard Bern come in at ten after twelve last night, but by then her dad was snoring on the couch and didn't even notice. Bern would tell him she got in at eleven thirty and he'd agree so he could pretend he wasn't passed out.

This place was so boring.

That girl Robyn would be waiting for her, but if she snuck out now she would be dead. There was never anything to do here. Bernie was boring. Summer was boring and the sun was out and the trailer was going to be really hot. Frankie turned on the counter fan and threw herself on the couch. It wasn't fair that Bern could do whatever she wanted but Frankie had to listen to everybody. And that girl Robyn was so pretty, too.

Under the coffee table was a boring kit her aunt Marie had sent her for Easter. Stupid funny face potholders she was supposed to make – instead of candy! Frankie pushed it under the couch where she wouldn't have to look at the stupid, boring thing again.

Everything was so, so, so, so, so boring.

She awoke to Bernadette, arms crossed and scowling. "Get off the couch," Bernie said.

Frankie stared back at her sister.

"You have ten minutes to get dressed and get out of here. If you're not back by four thirty I'll tell Dad you took off when I was in the bathroom. Again."

"I'll tell Dad you let me go."

"Go ahead. If you're willing to pay the price when Dad's at work."

"Why are you always so mean?"

"Nine minutes."

Frankie jumped up and ran to her room to change. She secured her holster around her hips, filled her metal canteen with water, grabbed the box of Cap'n Crunch and jumped out the door, letting it slam behind her.

"Don't be late, you little shit!" Bernadette called from the front step as she held a match to her first cigarette of the day.

Frankie looked at her watch: 10:35. She pulled the thongs from her feet and sped across the small patches of turf that marked the front of each mobile home, deftly leaping over gravel driveways and avoiding the sharp stones from the laneway. She was the Flash, fastest man alive, racing across the grass with an important message: I can come for lunch, Robyn, please wait. Please wait, please wait. She cut across the last yard, shot down the small embankment and into the open field, flying like a human helicopter across the meadow, sparing nothing in the race to reach her destination. Her feet were fleet and her lungs burst with purpose; the girl with the shiny braids and pink shorts was waiting, please, please God let her still be waiting. She said she would wait.

Child Care

As soon as Frankie was out of sight, Bernadette raced to the bathroom and retched. It had been at least two months since her last period, and despite fluttering and cramping in her gut she had not begun to bleed. A wave of nausea rose in her throat. She barfed into the toilet.

It was so unfair that it was hilarious. She'd done it with one guy – well, two, if you counted Leo Pyper, which she didn't being as it happened over a year ago, and Leo lived two lanes over with his wife, Darlene, and their baby, Matthew. Leo told her that Darlene wouldn't let him touch her, and Bernadette thought it seemed like a good idea to lose her virginity to a grown man as he would think about her needs first, which turned out to be mostly false because he came so fast. He tried to make it up to her but couldn't really because Darlene would be home with the baby soon and he had to shower and clean up the house. He gave her a pack of smokes for her trouble, warned her against Darlene's violent anger then asked if she was available to babysit the following Saturday, because he and Darlene would be going to a party. Bernadette told him sure. If the Pypers stayed out for eight hours they would give her a dollar bonus.

Leo tried to kiss her a couple more times, but Bernie politely declined. She told him she'd decided to save herself again until she got married. Leo laughed and said, "Well, you know where I live if you change your mind." But they moved out a few months later and that was the end of that.

So really, she only slept with one guy and they'd only done it three times and he'd always pulled out in time. She wasn't going to say anything to Mike, at least not until she got her period. Then she'd tell him how scared she was and that they'd have to lay off for a while because this was too close for comfort.

She lifted her head and puked again. Maybe the wieners and beans they'd had for supper last night were off. She rinsed her mouth then walked gingerly to the couch and lay down. She didn't even crave a cigarette.

Hostess

Frankie came upon Robyn sitting on a white flannel sheet spread out on the grass. A single yellow tin plate containing two peanut butter sandwiches sat in the middle of the blanket, two white paper napkins tucked neatly beneath. A red thermos stood beside the plate. At the top of the sheet sat a canvas knapsack, emptied and folding in on itself.

"You're just on time." Robyn stood up and brushed the front of her shorts (baby blue today) as if – impossibly – there might be crumbs on them. "I've prepared us lunch. I hope you like peanut butter sandwiches."

Frankie nodded.

"I see you've brought dessert, how thoughtful." Robyn reached for the box of Cap'n Crunch. "Here, let me take those from you."

"I have some water, too."

"We can drink it after we finish the Freshie. Do you like grape Freshie?"

Frankie nodded again.

"I can't imagine anyone not liking grape Freshie."

Frankie shook her head.

"Please, take a seat." Robyn turned her back and poured the Freshie into the thermos cup. "I hope you don't mind sipping from one cup. My mom wouldn't let me take another, but we can sip from opposite sides of the cup.

"I know it's not perfect. I just got my hostess badge, you know. I hosted a party with the kids in my class to celebrate the end of school and I sent out invitations and I planned the whole thing. We had Freshie – grape and cherry – and we put two quarters, four dimes, six nickels and ten pennies into the cake. So you see, if we were at my house I would have given us each a cup, and I thought of phoning you but I don't even know your last name –"

"Murray."

"I beg your pardon?"

"Murray is my last name."

"Oh." Robyn passed Frankie half a sandwich. "Here you are, Miss Murray."

"Thank you."

"My mom says it's good manners to use someone's name, then they know you've been listening."

Frankie chewed her sandwich and nodded.

"Freshie?" Robyn said.

Frankie took the cup from Robyn. "What's a hostess badge?"

Robyn chewed her bite quickly then cupped her hand over her mouth to speak. "I'm in Guides." She dropped her hand and, with her mouth closed, ran her tongue over her teeth. "I only have four badges, but I'm working on my fifth."

"Neat," Frankie said.

"I have Hostess, Singer, Reporter and Public Speaking." She took the cup from Frankie and sipped. "I'm working on my Camper badge, but it's not as easy as it sounds so I'm starting with Backyard Camper. Do you like camping, Frankie?"

"Sure," Frankie said. She'd only been camping once, two years ago at Castle Mountain, and Bern wouldn't talk and her dad snored and it was so cold in the morning she had to wear a toque and mitts. Still, there was a little creek and the trees smelled really good. There were chipmunks everywhere and a whisky jack, too. "But we didn't see a bear."

Robyn nodded with approval. "That's good."

"Don't you want to see a bear?"

"No!"

"I want to see a bear."

"What if it mauled you?"

Frankie shrugged. "Maybe from a car then."

"It's dangerous in the woods."

"Animals are more afraid of us than we are of them."

"Believe you me, I know all about the dangers of camping," Robyn said.

"You do?"

"I almost lost my eye."

"You did?"

"I snapped a dead branch from a tree, but it broke in two and one of the pieces flew into my eye and it swelled shut and looked terrible."

Frankie nodded and sipped the Freshie.

"Then, because my guide company was staying at Camp Bonita Glen – which is by where we used to live – and we had to sleep in tents, and I had this ring my half-brother Pete sent to me, and it was a silver flower, and I really liked it, and I thought I might lose it so I put it on my middle finger and I went to sleep and in the morning, when I woke up, my middle finger was so swollen that my mom had to take me to emergency to get the ring cut off. My dad came to get me because my mom wouldn't let me go back to camp. She said I was unfit, and that as captain of our company it wouldn't behoove her to show favouritism toward me.

"But she's not mad anymore because we had to move to Calgary. We're going to try backyard camping next month with Karen and Lisa, who are in our new Guide company."

"Neat," Frankie said.

"You're not one for words, are you?" Robyn asked.

Frankie blushed, "I guess not."

"Then we make a good pair, don't we? Because I'm a chatterbox and my mom says opposites attract."

Frankie smiled and reached for the cereal. "Are you ready for dessert?"

By noon the sun was sharp. The girls had packed up the plate and empty thermos and lay on the sheet, pulling up threads of grass and chewing on their soft white ends. Robyn chatted happily about Guides and badges. She petted her braids while she spoke, or waved her hands to make some point about the work that went into planning a year-end party when one of the boys – who nobody liked, really, but if you invite the whole class, you invite the whole class – was allergic to peanut butter, and she had planned on making peanut butter mini marshmallow squares with coloured marshmallows until his mom called.

Robyn's hands were so clean. Her pink nails grew just beyond the tips of her fingers. She wore tiny gold studs in her ears. Sometimes she would flick her pink tongue and lick the corner of her mouth, then she'd run her finger over the same spot. And she continued to talk while she fussed with her mouth, now about her brother Pete, who saw Pierre Trudeau in Toronto when he volunteered on the last election, but Margaret Trudeau wasn't there.

Robyn loved how the Trudeaus got married without anyone knowing. Her brother even saved her the *Toronto Daily Star* magazine with the Trudeaus' wedding photos. The bride wore a Moroccan caftan-style robe she made herself, but caftans are fitted at the waist so the dress wasn't technically a caftan. And there were daffodils, tulips, pussy willows – did Frankie like pussy willows? – and daisies on the altar. And daisies in Margaret's hair. Had Frankie seen the picture?

Frankie had seen the one where they were praying, but she'd hardly noticed, and her dad had snorted and said Trudeau was a lucky old duck, even young girls loved the bastard. Her dad voted Liberal once but now said, "Fool me once shame on you, fool me twice shame on me." But Trudeau won anyway, and then her dad said, "What was the point when Ontario and Quebec always decided the elections?"

Frankie's life was boring; she'd never been farther east than Moose Jaw. Her mom took her there when Frankie was six to see her aunt Marie, whose husband, Archie, was stationed there. It was so hot they went to the outdoor pool and Bern jumped off the high diving board, but Frankie wasn't allowed. Now her aunt and uncle were in a place called Trenton, and it's too far to go and they have no reason to visit now because Frankie's dad never had the time of day for her uncle who, Jimmy said, was a mean bastard. But Robyn used to live in Toronto and even got to stay in a motel on a lake with a swing set and a dock. And she went to Disneyland, too.

Robyn's voice carried up high and then fell down quiet when she caught her breath or had a thought about which direction to go in her talking. It was the most Frankie had heard spoken in three years, or maybe her whole life because she couldn't remember if her mom talked or just read her books from the library.

Robyn realized the time and jumped up with a start. "I'm going to be dead!"

Frankie helped Robyn, who was supposed to be home in ten minutes, gather her gear. She had to get her eyes checked, not that there was anything wrong with them, but every year her mother got them tested just to be safe. And sometimes she got her hearing checked, too.

"You haven't told me anything about you," Robyn said.

Frankie shrugged, "I can show you the gophers."

"Are you a hunter?"

"I'm a tracker."

"You stalk the gophers?"

"I follow them, if that's what you mean," Frankie said. "But you have to be quiet."

Robyn blushed. "I know I talk too much."

Then Frankie blushed. "No! I mean you have to walk quiet. I'll show you."

"I'll come tomorrow at the same time," Robyn said. "Unless I'm grounded, then I'll come the next day. Unless I'm still grounded. Do you mind checking?"

Frankie shook her head.

Robyn stuck her left hand toward Frankie. "Let's shake on it."

Frankie reached out with her right hand.

"No!" Robyn said. "The secret Guide shake. Use your left hand."

Robyn clasped Frankie's left hand in hers and shook vigorously. Then she ran across the grass toward the man-made lake and her new house, her braids bouncing across her shoulders. Frankie placed her hand on the hilt of her gun, drew it quickly from the holster and spun in a circle, checking for bandits. She slung her canteen over her shoulder and looked east; Robyn had disappeared from view. Frankie sauntered toward home; she had never seen a man-made lake, but she wouldn't mind giving it a try.

Homemaker

Jimmy looked at his watch; it was ten minutes to six. The girls were going to be hungry. He had half a pint left then he'd grab a bucket of chicken on the way home. The waitress walked past with a tray full of draft. He liked the way her denim blouse pulled apart when she held the tray to her shoulder. A guy could catch a look at her white bra if he wasn't too obvious.

He figured her to be in her late twenties – too young for an old fart, but not hard on the eyes, not hard at all. She wore her hair long under a light pink cowboy hat. And he liked her short little jean skirt, too. Barb might have had a thing or two to say about the length of her hem, but Jimmy wasn't complaining. The girl caught him looking her way and held his eyes. Jimmy's cheeks burned and she smiled brightly then turned on her heel to drop some beers off at the table to his right.

The bar was jumping. They were midway through Stampede and work everywhere was booming. The folks here had money to burn and were in full party mode. No one but Jimmy seemed worried about kids or supper plans. And, Jesus, what was left for him for the rest of the night? A little TV until he passed out plus two daughters who were as strange to him as foreign countries. He'd just like a little break, if that wasn't asking too much.

Jimmy lifted his hand toward the waitress and held up two fingers. She dropped two more half pints at his table and winked. He lit up a smoke, pushed back his chair and walked to the pay phone. The girls could open a can of spaghetti tonight.

Friend to Animals

 Robyn didn't return until Monday, five days after their picnic lunch. By then, Frankie had decided that the strange, tidy girl would never return. Even so, each day – except for the rainy day after their picnic – Frankie made her way through the grass, toward the cluster of skinny trees with her canteen filled with water and a peanut butter sandwich packed in the Crown Royal bag looped carefully around her holster.

On Monday, Robyn was standing in the grass looking in Frankie's direction. She waved her arms madly when Frankie came into view then ran toward her friend.

"I was afraid you'd be mad," Robyn said.

"I brought a peanut butter sandwich."

"I wasn't grounded yesterday, but Sunday we go to church."

Frankie's dad didn't make them go to Mass anymore, thank Christ, because Mass was boring as hell.

"I only brought an apple," Robyn said. "Because my mom thinks I'm at the lake. She doesn't want me out in the blazing sun in the middle of nowhere."

"Actually, there's a lot of gophers living out here," Frankie said.

Robyn nodded. "So, you know how to stalk quarry?"

"What?" Frankie said.

"You know, you creep up on the gopher, without being seen, heard or smelled. So you can observe them."

"Sometimes." Frankie had hardly been able to creep up on the gophers, although sometimes, if she stayed calm and quiet, they didn't seem to mind her being there. She knew a lot about gophers, but most of it was from the encyclopedia in the library, not from watching them in real life, no matter how hard she tried.

Robyn nodded. "Maybe you want to teach me how," she said. "So I can get my stalking badge."

"Okay."

Robyn licked her finger and held it up to the wind. "Which way is the wind blowing?"

"I don't worry about that," Frankie said. "The gophers are kind of used to me."

"My dad says they're prairie dogs."

"They're not dogs."

"You know a lot about gophers."

"I wish I was a gopher."

Robyn laughed. "You don't like being a girl?"

Frankie shrugged. "Follow me." They walked beyond the small copse of poplars, away from the new construction invading the grassland. Frankie pulled the thongs off her feet and tucked them into her back pocket.

"You don't want to make any noise." Frankie pointed to the navy canvas sneakers on Robyn's feet.

Robyn shook her head. "My mom would kill me."

"Just make sure you don't make noise," Frankie said. She walked carefully into the field. "They're over here," she whispered, and crouched down on her haunches. She scanned the prairie looking for a flash of tan fur. The boy gophers were gone now. Girl gophers stayed with their moms forever.

Robyn squatted beside her. A ground squirrel raced across the grass and jumped into a burrow. Robyn squeezed Frankie's forearm and smiled widely. She was the prettiest girl Frankie had ever seen, but if they were gophers Frankie would have to fight her and live with Bernadette instead, because that's what gophers do. They live near their moms and fight the girls they're not related to, even if they are friends.

At first, her dad said Mom went away, then he said she went to sleep, and then he said she went to Heaven and he cried and a bubble of snot came out of his nose and popped. Just like gum. Bernadette jumped up and down on the spot and said, no no no no. And Frankie cried, not because her mom was in Heaven but because her dad had snot running down his face. At first Frankie thought her mom would come back down from Heaven, at bedtime or something, and they would say a Hail Mary and kiss goodnight.

But that was stupid. People don't come down from Heaven. Except for the Virgin Mary sometimes. Maybe a saint could come down from Heaven, but you couldn't really be a saint if you had babies.

Her mom wore navy or brown slacks and, Frankie remembered, a yellow blouse. She'd had an apron that went over her shirt, and she liked *The Tommy Hunter Show* because Tommy Hunter was a classy guy. Frankie thought Tommy Hunter was so boring, but they don't watch him anymore.

Frankie can't think what her mom smelled like. She asked her dad once and he said, "Dammit, Frankie, she smelled like a thirty-eight-year-old woman, what kind of a question is that?" And

Bernadette said, "Not like you, fart face." Animals know everything because of smell, but Frankie knows nothing.

Frankie leaned toward Robyn and inhaled deeply. Robyn smelled green. They could be cousins and live close together. Or sisters, except Frankie had a sister and sisters were mean. A gopher came out of its hole and looked them in the eye. Frankie smiled but didn't show her teeth so she didn't seem like a threat. She held the eye of the gopher. Robyn's fingers dug into her arm.

"He's so cute," she hissed.

"She," Frankie said.

"She," Robyn said.

The gopher popped back underground, and Frankie pulled out her sandwich and took a bite then passed it to Robyn. Robyn turned the sandwich to the bottom end and took a bite then passed it back to Frankie. They waited for the gophers to return.

When it became evident that the gophers would not be returning, the girls wandered back toward the shade of the trees. Frankie showed Robyn how to whistle with a piece of grass between her thumbs, but Robyn couldn't do it. Frankie showed Robyn how to fart with her armpit, but Robyn couldn't do that either.

Robyn's problem was she was a city girl. She told Frankie that she hadn't lived near gophers or big empty fields in Toronto; she'd lived near houses and apartment buildings. Robyn picked a dandelion puff, made a wish and blew the ripe weed apart.

Frankie told Robyn that gophers were all girls after mating season, that they were sisters and mothers and aunts and grandmas, so they were probably cousins, too. Frankie said they could pretend they were cousins so they didn't have to be enemies, because gophers fought their enemies.

Robyn told Frankie she couldn't get dirty though.

Creative Drama

Bernadette sat on the trunk of Mike Walsh's white Falcon. He pressed himself between her legs and reached his hand up under her shirt. Her breasts bloomed under his touch. She reached for the back of his head and knitted her fingers into his hair, he touched her lips with his tongue and she opened her mouth. In a year, Mike would head off to university to study engineering, like his father and grandfather had done. He said he wanted to marry her when he finished.

Bernadette pushed Mike away and jumped off of the trunk. "I'm late," she said.

"For what? I thought your dad was home."

"My period is late."

She heard Mike suck in his breath.

"And I'm puking."

"Shit," he said.

Bernadette watched Mike chew on his lips, struck silent. His nose was burned from his landscaping job, his strawberry-blond hair bleached almost white. He was tall and sweet and everyone thought she was lucky to get him. His dad was a regular usher at Mass; his mom was secretary-treasurer for the CWL. Mike had two older sisters, one who was married and one who was a nurse, and a fourteen-year-old brother. Every Sunday the whole family ate dinner at his house, even his married sister. Mike's life was like a frigging TV show.

"I could work on the rigs," he said. "My folks will be mad." He was pacing in a circle. "But they'll settle down after we're married."

Bernadette felt a surge of anger snap behind her eyes. "Who said I was going to marry you?"

"What?" he asked.

"Who said I was even going to keep it?" She hated his friendly parents and Sunday dinners. "Who said it was even yours?"

Mike licked his lips. "What?"

"I don't know who the father is," she said.

Mike swallowed and looked away.

Bernadette was sick of doing what people thought she should do. And even if she wouldn't have said so yesterday, today it was true; she didn't want to marry Mike. She didn't want a husband and four kids, and she was sick of God and the Catholic Church. She started to cry. Chagrined, she stamped her foot in the dust. "I don't," she said. "I don't know who the father is."

They drove back into town in silence. Before getting into the car, Mike said, "But I thought you loved me," and Bernadette shrugged her shoulders. She supposed she might still get her period; stranger things had happened. But she wasn't going to marry Mike Walsh, that was for sure. His cheeks were red with the effort of not talking. He hung his arm out of the driver's window and tapped on the door. Bernadette almost felt bad for him then figured he'd get over it after a few Sunday dinners and a night out with Cathy Currie, who was dying to get her hands on Mike and he knew it.

Not that he'd ever done anything to provoke it, Bernadette had to give him that, but it's not as if he had nowhere to turn.

When he pulled into the trailer park, Mike whispered, "What are you going to do?"

"Give it away." Bernadette surprised herself with her certainty. "Unless I get my period," she said.

Mike nodded. "Good luck, Bernie."

"Don't you worry about me," she said and closed the door behind her. Bernadette watched Mike drive away. But it was true: she couldn't marry him, she didn't want to. She didn't want to marry Mike Walsh and join the Catholic Women's League. She didn't want to have a baby or a little sister that she had to take care of. She didn't want to finish school and she didn't want to live here in a fucking trailer court. She didn't want to puke and get fat. She didn't want to think about her mother. She didn't want anything anymore, but she wanted something else.

Cook

Jimmy Murray looked at his daughters: Bernadette pushed her pork chop around the plate with a fork while Frances kept her head bent over the table and shoved pieces of meat into her mouth faster than she could chew. If Jimmy had been sullen at the table growing up he'd have been knocked across the room with one well-aimed smack from his father's hand. He wouldn't have stomped out of the house, or leaned on his elbows, shovelling food into his mouth.

"Slow down!" Jimmy placed his hand on Frankie's arm.

She raised her head and said, with her mouth full, "I'm hungry."

Bernadette snorted.

"You're going to make yourself sick," Jimmy said.

"A wild animal has to eat quickly or it will perish," Frankie answered.

"Well good thing you're a tame girl then. Finish one bite before you start the next. And sit up straight."

Frankie straightened up, put her fork down and glared at her father. He was sure he'd read in one of those lady magazines in the doctor's office that supper was the time for a family to talk about their day. But Jimmy didn't have a clue what to say. He sighed and looked back at his plate. He was cook and chief bottle washer serving up crappy suppers to two silent girls who wanted nothing to do with him. King of the castle? The joke was on Jimmy.

Frankie was now pointedly chewing her food in exaggerated chomps.

"Jesus, chew with your mouth closed," Bernadette snapped.

"Language," Jimmy said.

If Barb were here, they would have been talking. By now they would have moved to Strathmore and been running a little farm. That was the dream he and Barb had shared: a quarter section, a horse, a dog and a field of crops. But the savings were gone now. Jimmy took a little time off work after Barb passed – to see that the girls got the hang of doing things on their own. Then he took fewer hours to get home earlier and found that a few drinks at the bar helped with the echoing absence of Barb.

Bernadette pushed her chair from the table and stood up.

"I can't eat with a little pig chewing next to me," she said and left the table.

Frankie watched her sister march into the bathroom and lock the door behind her. She closed her mouth. Jimmy sighed and squeezed his forehead. Frankie turned and watched the evening breeze gust against the living room curtain, lifting the blue cotton and then letting it fall again against the screen.

Jimmy placed his hand on Frankie's arm. "How about I take you to the Dairy Queen for a dipped cone?" he asked.

Inside the bathroom Bernadette turned the taps on full blast then retched into the toilet. She splashed her face with water, lay on her back on the floor and closed her eyes. With luck they'd give her ten minutes of peace.

Interpreter

There are two dreams that regularly populate the sleep of Jimmy Murray. In the first Barb is annoyed with him. "But you're dead," he says to her, "everyone thinks you're dead. We had a funeral." Barbara is not happy. She's tired of picking up after him, she says, can't he help her sometimes? She knows he works hard, but so does she. "Just pick up your socks and hang up your towels," she tells him. Jimmy tries to tell Barbara that everyone thinks she's dead, but she won't listen. Then he wakes up. He wakes up and lays there in the dark double bed. He spreads his legs to prove to himself that he is alone and then he pulls himself in close, turns on his side and looks toward the wall in the dark. He can't see anything, really, and that helps.

In the second dream Barb is on a gurney. She is bloody. Jimmy is crying, even though he should be strong. Barb looks at him. He doesn't say it out loud, but he thinks it. He thinks: I thought you already died; I thought this was over. Barb looks like hell; her skin is grey and her eyes unfocused. Everything hurts her, even when he brushes her hair across her forehead. She raises her hand to his and says, "Don't, Jimmy, please." The last thing Jimmy wants to do is to hurt Barb. And so, he stands beside her bed and waits for her to die.

After he wakes from the second dream Jimmy turns on the light. On those nights there is no return to sleep. Instead Jimmy gets up, lights a cigarette and boils water for a cup of Nescafé. On those nights he moves to the armchair in the living room and sits and smokes and drinks coffee until the new day begins. When he hears the newspaper hit the porch, he grabs it and moves to the kitchen table and flips through the news of the day, scanning headlines and articles and trying like hell to avoid the stories that cause him to worry he's going to raise two sex- or drug-crazed girls. If that happens ... The anxiety rises up his throat like bile; it makes him want to start his day with a good stiff drink.

Home Defence

Bernadette rolled over in bed. According to the glow-in-the-dark hands on her alarm clock it was quarter after four in the morning. She could hear her dad shuffling around the kitchen; smell his cigarette. She traced her finger across the wooden slats of the top bunk. The clock ticked loudly, but Frankie's breathing was deep. It made Bernie want to be little again and free of worry, like her sister.

Bernadette placed her hand on her tummy, above her uterus, above the fruit of her womb.

"Hello," she whispered.

Yesterday afternoon she'd gone to Dr. Cooper. It wasn't as if she didn't already know; she just needed him to tell her how long she had. After he examined her, Dr. Cooper told her she could expect to deliver a baby early in February.

He asked her what she planned to do. Bernadette shrugged. She said she'd figure something out. He asked her who the father was. Bernadette whispered, "I don't know." She blushed. Dr. Cooper sucked in his breath and sighed. He told her she should find some place to go – did she want him to recommend a home? But Bernie didn't want him to do that, so she told him no, and he told her it wouldn't be easy to stay home, people would talk. Bernadette nodded. "You'll have to tell your father," he told her. Bernadette nodded. He patted her hand and said he was sorry. Bernadette thanked him.

Now there was no more hoping.

In the kitchen, the kettle whistled and Jimmy promptly lifted it from the burner. Bernadette rolled toward the wall. Last year, Carole Fortier had suddenly left school in January. Supposedly she'd gone off to help her aunt in Regina, but everyone knew the real reason she was gone. It was anybody's guess who the father was. Or it was Scott Daly; it was probably Scott Daly. He was an asshole of the first order and definitely wouldn't have offered to marry Carole. Maybe Carole stupidly thought getting pregnant was a way to keep Scott.

Bernadette's throat tightened. She squeezed her eyes shut. Her mom would say there was no use crying over spilt milk. Or her mom would throw her out.

Maybe she would try jumping off a fence, maybe that would work. "Please, God," she whispered. "Please, God, let me get my period." She repeated the mantra in her head – please, God, please, God, please, God – until she fell back to sleep.

In the morning, Bern sent Frankie away, no questions asked, with instructions to return before Jimmy got home from work. First Bernadette tried a scalding bath. She emerged red and excruciated but not bleeding. She walked out looking for a fence that seemed perilous enough but the trailer park had none. She considered jumping off of Mr. Moreland's storage shed but it was smooth and tall with no grips for climbing. Anyway, Mrs. Moreland spent most of her day standing in the kitchen window, smoking and surveying the trailer park with a sour look on her face.

Bernadette returned, defeated, to the trailer. She slumped on the front steps and lit a cigarette. She let it burn between her fingers, watched the smoke trail toward the sky and dashed the ashes. But, beyond lighting the cigarette, she was unable to tolerate her favourite pastime. Bernadette was totally screwed, in every sense of the word.

She could see, in the distance, Frankie walking toward the trailer with another girl behind her. Frankie had some nerve, bringing a strange kid around. Frankie, who had never before, in all her life, mentioned a friend, was bringing some kid home when she was supposed to stay out of Bernadette's hair. Bernie pinched her cigarette then tossed it into the gravel. She stood up, brushed the grit off the back of her legs and went inside. She could stand a little bit of chicken noodle soup anyway.

Folklore

By the time the girls came through the door Bernadette had the soup warming on the stove. She was sitting at the table casually flipping through the television guide. Bernadette licked her finger and turned the page, engrossed.

Frankie said, "Hi."

Bernadette lifted her head. Frankie's friend was wearing a green gingham short suit and her hair was plaited like *Rebecca of Sunnybrook Farm*. Where on Earth did Frankie find her? The girl waved her fingers at Bernadette. Bernadette waved her fingers at the girl.

"You going to introduce us?" she asked Frankie.

"I'm Robyn," the girl piped up.

"I'm Bernadette."

"My big sister," Frankie said.

"Where's your mom?" Robyn asked.

"Heaven. We think." Bernadette winked.

Robyn's cheeks turned bright pink.

"You didn't say," Robyn said to Frankie.

"I was going to," Frankie said.

"What are you guys doing?" Bernadette asked.

Frankie shrugged. She looked away from Bernadette, nervous. Bernadette's interest was piqued. Frankie never had friends. Well, none worth knowing anyway.

"Where do you live?" she asked Robyn.

"In Bonavista," Robyn said.

"You're here instead of at the lake?"

Robyn nodded.

Stupid kid. Bernadette filled a bowl with soup and broke a handful of soda crackers into the dish. She carefully tasted the soup and sat for a moment with her eyes closed, biting back nausea. When she opened her eyes, the two girls remained fixed in their spots, staring at her.

"What are you looking at?" she asked.

"Nothing," Frankie said. "Want some soup?" she asked Robyn.

Robyn sat down beside Bernadette. "Yes please."

Frankie passed a bowl and crackers to Robyn then joined her at the table. She lifted a noodle with her spoon and sucked it down her throat. Robyn covered her mouth with her hand and giggled.

It was stifling in the trailer, even with the door open. Bernadette pushed her bowl away; already the smell was getting to her. Frankie and her friend were talking quickly. Bernadette carried her bowl to the sink. The girls chattered on, oblivious to Bernadette, oblivious to the heat. Bernadette went out to the steps and lit a cigarette.

She closed her eyes against the sun. She laid her body across the steps like Jesus on the cross. She tried to imagine spikes being nailed into her hands, then lifted them over her head and pressed the lit end of her smoke into her left palm. Her hand flinched, but she held it firmly against the burning cherry, a spike being driven through her palm. And like Christ, she didn't complain.

Bernadette let her arms fall back and spread wide again. Mike would go on to university in a year, her dad would still go to work,

Frankie would start junior high and they would all think that it was normal; they wouldn't even notice how she had suffered for their sins. "Father, forgive them, they know not what they do," she whispered. Her left hand throbbed.

Bernadette could relate to Jesus. Forced to do everything for everyone else. Forced to not have a life. It was stupid to be Bernie and it was stupid to be Jesus. What she didn't get is why he just didn't take off with Mary Magdalene and go live in Bethlehem or some other place, where no one gave a crap about what he did. Where no one even knew who he was. Instead, he just suffered. Idiot.

Signaller

Frankie lay with her head hanging off the edge of the top bunk and watched Robyn spell the alphabet with her fingers.

She held up her hand. Her thumb was tucked behind her ring and pinky fingers; her index and middle fingers were held horizontally. "What's this?" Robyn asked.

"G?"

"No, G is this." Robyn closed her middle finger so only one finger was left pointing. "That was H."

"H," Frankie said.

"That's right," Robyn nodded. "I'll draw them for you and it'll help you to remember. And then we can talk privately."

"How about ig-pay atin-lay?" Frankie asked.

"Too many people know it."

"I guess."

"Just follow my hands and you'll get it eventually."

Frankie copied Robyn and, as they slowly moved through the alphabet, Frankie let her thoughts drift.

If Robyn was Frankie's blood sister and they were gophers then they could live in the same territory. Bernadette wasn't even any fun anymore and Robyn was kind of an only child. They should become blood sisters. Unless Robyn was afraid of cutting herself.

"Pay attention!" Robyn said.

"We should be blood sisters," Frankie said.

Robyn smiled. "Okay."

Frankie pulled a penknife out of her pocket. "We can do it now." She jumped off the bunk and opened her penknife. "I'll start." She poked the knife into her left index finger. A small bead of blood popped out of her fingertip.

Robyn took the knife from Frankie and poked her own left index finger. "Dammit, that hurts," she hissed. The two girls pressed their fingers together. Robyn laughed and shook her head.

Junior Camper

Her dad was snoring on the couch, but each time Frankie tried to change the channel he lifted up his head and said, "Leave it!" Baseball was stupid. If her dad were a gopher he'd be running for his life, because that's how it was for boy gophers. If he were a gopher, she wouldn't even know who he was and she'd be able to fight him.

But then she'd be living with Bernie.

Bernie wouldn't let her in the room. She was lying in bed listening to the radio and she said Frankie couldn't come in. She said Frankie smelled and needed a bath and her dad said yes, she did, but then he fell asleep on the couch and didn't even make her. Anyway, Frankie didn't care if she smelled. Animals smelled; that's just the way it was. Get used to it.

Bernie smelled, too, sometimes. "Yes, but then I have a bath," Bernie said, and Frankie copied her in a squeaky voice and Bernie punched her arm and Jimmy yelled at them to settle down. Then Bernie ran into their room and slammed the door, and Jimmy said,

"Do you have to antagonize her?" But nobody ever said the same thing to Bernie. It wasn't fair.

Frankie went to the porch. It was nine and the sun had moved close to the mountains. The sky was still bright but losing its warmth. Frankie liked this time of day, when the crickets sang and you could hear lawn mowers and kids calling. It was like living in a gopher town: you knew people were around and you knew they would warn you if danger was present, but you stayed in your own tunnel and listened to the ruckus.

Frankie liked the feel of the hard wood porch pressing against her head. The wood was still a little warm. A mosquito buzzed overhead and she clapped it between her hands. Dead little bloodsucker.

"Let that be a warning to all of you," she said. Then she gave her evil laugh.

Frankie was never going to bathe, unless her dad made her. She liked smelling like a gopher. Robyn didn't say she stunk, so Bernie was just being a bitch. That was the sad truth: Bernie was a bitch and her dad didn't care. She wished she could be adopted because she hated them as much as they hated her. That was the sad truth, too.

"Jesus Christ!"

Frankie's dad was standing over her.

"Have you been here all night?"

Frankie had been dreaming that a bad guy was spraying her with air from a fridge that was making her stick to a wall. Her arms and legs ached.

"Get in the goddamn house," Jimmy said.

Frankie sat up and rubbed the sleep from her eyes. The sky was light. "What time is it?"

"It's six thirty in the bloody morning." Her dad was angry. "What were you thinking?"

"It was an accident," Frankie said.

"An accident is when you drive your car into a stop sign," Jimmy said. "Or you drop a plate. Sleeping on the porch is not an accident."

Frankie stood up. "Nothing happened," she said.

Jimmy propped a cigarette between his lips. "Just get inside, Frankie." He lit the smoke and, on his exhalation, said, "And try to get along with your sister, would you?"

Frankie walked into the trailer, stuck her tongue out at the wall, flopped onto the couch and fell back asleep.

Stalker

The gophers were boring and wouldn't come out of their burrows. Frankie and Robyn lay on the prickly grass looking at the sky, trying to see the bend of the Earth, but the sky was flat as a pancake.

"It's flat as a pancake," Frankie said.

"Flat as my chest."

Frankie turned her head toward Robyn. It was true; Robyn didn't have any boobs at all. Frankie placed her hands on her own chest; she had two little bumps the size of apricots.

"Your chest is nice," Frankie said.

"Yours is better."

"I guess," Frankie muttered.

Robyn took Frankie's hand in hers and held it up toward the sun. "Blood sisters," she said.

Frankie tightened her hand around Robyn's and shook their combined fist at the sun. They lay still with their arms raised until Robyn's arm began to tremble with the effort. Frankie loosened her grip and Robyn let her arm flop to the grass.

"I'm a weakling," Robyn said.

Frankie let her hand drop on top of Robyn's and the girls twined their fingers.

"Yeah, but you're smart," Frankie said. "You speak sign language."

"And a little bit of French, s'il vous plait," Robyn said.

The girls continued to stare at the sky in silence. A light breeze blew across their faces; the grass flickered. They had eaten sandwiches and now the long, unpromising afternoon stretched out before them.

"I'm never going to get my stalking badge," Robyn said.

It was true. Things weren't looking good. The gophers were more cautious with the two of them about. There were no other animals.

Once, Frankie had seen a coyote, but that was last spring and it was from a distance. The coyote was heading away, farther into the grassland, beyond the development. Frankie would have liked to bring it home as a pet, but her dad said absolutely no dogs, he had his hands full enough already.

"We can stalk Bernie," Frankie suggested.

"Doesn't she just sit in your house?"

"Sometimes she goes out to smoke," Frankie said. "We can count her smokes. And if we go behind the trailer, we can hear her through the window. She talks on the phone a lot. She has a boyfriend."

"What do they do?"

"They make out in the kitchen."

"Is he cute?"

"No!" Frankie said. "I don't know. Maybe."

"Okay," Robyn said.

They made their way toward the trailer park in silence. The skin on Frankie's nose was tight, burned by the midday sun. She glanced at Robyn. Her nose was red, too. And the hair at the back of her head had escaped the tight braids. Even with messy hair, Robyn was prettier than anybody.

Frankie wasn't pretty, but she didn't care. Bernie was always wearing eyeshadow and mascara, and she got mad if Frankie touched it. Like she was going to wear it. As if.

"But we'll have to be very quiet," Frankie told Robyn. "Bernie is like a cat, she hears everything. Unless you're extremely super quiet."

L-E-T-S S-I-G-N, Robyn spelled with her fingers.

Y-E-S, Frankie spelled back.

S-H-A-K-E. Robyn stopped and thrust her left hand toward Frankie.

Frankie grasped her hand in their secret shake.

The girls crept toward the Murray's trailer, crouched low, silent and moving toward their prey.

Robyn gave Frankie the thumbs-up.

There was a white car parked in front of their trailer. Frankie tapped Robyn's arm. M-I-K-E, she spelled.

Robyn mouthed the word *boyfriend*?

Frankie nodded. She signalled Robyn to follow her to the back of the trailer, near the open kitchen window. Bernadette liked to sit on the kitchen counter with Mike standing between her legs. All they did was kiss, and sometimes Mike would put his hand up Bernie's shirt and Bernie would giggle and move in closer until you couldn't see his arm at all. But it was boring. If you asked Frankie, it was just stupid.

There was a garbage can under the window. Frankie helped Robyn climb up and peek through the window. Robyn flashed two thumbs-up then dropped down quickly, a finger pressed to her lips, ssshhh. The girls held their breath while the tap was turned on and then off.

"You'd better just go," Bernie said.

"I know it's mine," Mike said.

"No, Mike," Bernadette said. "It's mine."

"We can do this together." He sounded like he was going to cry.

"Not in your life."

"But I love you." His voice actually cracked.

"You don't know anything," Bernie said.

"Please!"

Bernie snapped, "I hate this baby, Mike, and whether or not you believe it, I wish I'd never met you. And when it's born, I'm getting rid of it. And you have no say, because I'm the one who's going to get fat and ugly and push out a baby, not you. So get the fuck out of my house."

Robyn and Frankie stared at one another. They heard footsteps and then the screen door slam. Frankie sprinted to the side of the trailer; Mike hopped into his car and peeled out of the driveway, sending gravel flying. Bernadette stood on the porch with her arms crossed. She looked to the right and saw Frankie watching the car pull away.

"You fucking brat," she hissed. "Say anything and I'll beat the shit out of you." She turned on her heel and marched into the trailer. "And don't think of coming inside!" she called.

Frankie could feel Robyn breathing behind her.

"I'd better go home," Robyn whispered.

Frankie nodded. "Yeah."

"I'll see you tomorrow?"

"Okay."

"Okay."

Frankie watched Robyn run across the trailer park toward the new roads and the big houses and the pretty lake. She was supposed to go to Robyn's house tomorrow, for lunch and a swim in the man-made lake. Frankie dropped slowly onto the stair of the porch. Her stomach felt like it was full of wasps.

Little House Emblem

Frankie woke in the dark. A fist banged against the table. And then crying.

"Bernie?" Frankie whispered. No answer. Once her eyes adjusted to the dark, she hung her head over the side of the bunk. Bernadette's bed was empty. Frankie lay back and strained to listen: she heard Bernadette's voice but the words were unclear. Frankie crept from her bed and quietly turned the door handle; through the crack of the door she could see her father crying at the table, fat tears running down his face. Bernadette sat across from him, also crying. Frankie scrambled back up the top bunk and turned to face the door, opened just wide enough to see her dad. She could hear them if she lay quietly.

"What did you expect would happen?" he asked.

"I didn't think it was that easy." There was a silence, then Bernie added, "I didn't think God would let something terrible happen to us again."

"Well that's piss-poor logic," Jimmy said. "Your mother must be rolling in her grave." He pulled a hankie out of his pocket and blew his nose. "Who's the father?"

"I'm not sure."

Jimmy jumped up, "You're not sure?" His face was red. He raised his hand toward Bernadette and Frankie sucked in her breath. Then Jimmy slumped back into his chair and dropped his forehead into his palm. Bernadette remained silent.

"Go to bed," he said. "Just go to bed."

Frankie heard the scraping sound of the chair being pushed back. Bernadette walked into their room a moment later. She stared at Frankie and Frankie looked right back at her, then Bernadette pushed the door closed and crawled into the lower bunk.

"I mean it, Frankie. Say anything I don't want him to know and I'll beat the living shit out of you," Bernadette said.

"I won't."

"You'd better not."

Frankie rolled toward the wall. She squeezed back tears. The last thing she wanted was for Bernie to hear her crying.

Rescuer

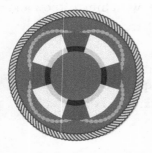

Jimmy poured a glass of rye, lit a cigarette and inhaled deeply. He rubbed his face dry with a dishtowel then let it drop to the floor. He squeezed the end of his nose between his fingers and wiped the snot on his jeans. Then he punched his fist through the wall panelling. It hurt more than he had expected, the contact of his knuckles with the thin wall.

He was going to have to send Bernie away. He'd have to call Marie – she had a couple of kids now, maybe she could use some help – and there'd be no harm in the cousins getting to know each other, if Marie could abide with housing a pregnant girl. Who knew what her jackass of a husband would say, but Jimmy had nowhere else to turn. He swallowed a sob with a mouthful of rye.

He looked at his watch. Well he couldn't call Trenton now – it was after one in the morning out there – but he wasn't going to be sleeping any time soon. He reached up to the counter and pulled the bottle of rye down onto his lap.

Attendance

In the morning Frankie crept out of her room with her swimsuit tucked under her arm. Bernadette was sleeping with her mouth slightly open, little gusts of air popping between her lips. In the living room Frankie pulled on her swimsuit and a pair of cut-offs. She ate a bowl of Rice Krispies, liberally sprinkled with sugar, then ran a brush through her hair, and rolled a towel and placed it on the table. She looked at the clock; it was quarter to nine. Robyn didn't expect her until eleven. Frankie lay on the couch, her hands folded neatly across her chest. It was going to take a long time to get to eleven.

Frankie startled awake two hours later when Bernadette slammed the bathroom door. She grabbed her towel and raced to her bike. She pedalled furiously toward Lake Bonavista but then slowed and slipped off her bike as she approached Robyn's address. Frankie knew the houses in Bonavista were big, but Robyn never said her house was massive.

The driveway was paved and led to a dark brown double garage that was wider than the Murray's trailer. The rest of the house stretched out beside the garage. There were three angular windows that sloped and gave view to a vaulted ceiling and Frankie could see the side of a brick fireplace. The house was split-level and above the garage were windows that led to more rooms. No one Frankie knew lived in a house like Robyn's. Frankie dropped her bike onto the front lawn and rang the doorbell.

A thin, blonde woman opened the door. She wore a lime green sleeveless top and a green-and-white-checked skirt that landed two inches above the knee. There were four neat white buttons down the centre of her skirt. She wore white sandals, a large white bangle on her left wrist and her hair was cut in short layers that curled around her face. She looked like a movie star.

"Hello," she said. "Frankie?"

Frankie, awestruck and speechless, nodded affirmatively.

"I'm Mrs. Oliver." She gave Frankie a quick glance. "How about you walk around the side of the house and meet Robyn in the yard."

Frankie nodded again, crossed the driveway and turned behind the garage, heading toward the yard. She heard the front door close behind her.

"Frankie!" Robyn squealed and ran toward her. "I thought you'd never get here." She pulled Frankie into the yard; the lawn was thick under their feet. A short wooden dock stretched over the water. There was a lounge chair and a large wooden picnic table. Two girls sat at the table watching Robyn and Frankie.

"That's Karen and that's Lisa," said Robyn. "They go to Guides." Both girls, like Robyn, had long, light hair tied back neatly in single ponytails. One wore a terry cloth shift over her bathing suit, the other, a gingham sundress. Robyn's skirt was made of fabric that matched her bathing suit. Frankie stuffed her hands into the pockets of her cut-offs.

"This is Frankie," Robyn said.

"You have a boy's name?" the girl called Lisa asked.

"My name is Frances."

"It still sounds like a boy's name," said Lisa.

"Robyn sounds like a boy's name," said Robyn.

"No, it doesn't," said Lisa.

"Christopher Robin," said Robyn.

"Hot dogs!" Robyn's mom called as she walked out the glass sliding doors carrying a wooden tray with four hot dogs, four stacked plastic glasses, a jar of mustard and a bottle of ketchup.

"Thank you, Mrs. Oliver," Karen and Lisa sang in unison.

Mrs. Oliver looked at Frankie. "The girls have been hungry waiting for you. You don't mind starting with lunch now?"

Frankie shook her head.

"Good then," she said. "I'll be right back with the Freshie."

When Mrs. Oliver returned, she had a plastic jug filled with red Freshie in one hand and a glass tumbler filled with clear liquid and a piece of lime in the other. She placed the pitcher on the table then sat on the lounge chair. She lit a cigarette, leaned back into the chair and sipped her drink.

Robyn and her friends chattered on about the temperature of the water (cold) and the Freshie (yummy) and teachers (mean, mostly). Frankie chewed on her hot dog, silent and nervous. She had expected only Robyn. They wouldn't be allowed to swim for an hour after eating and Frankie couldn't think of what she might say between now and then.

They were going to suntan on the dock. Frankie followed obediently, lunch churning in her belly. The girls pulled off their dresses, revealing brightly coloured two-piece bathing suits. Frankie wore a plain red one-piece she had inherited from her sister. It was faded and out of date, but before now it had never bothered her. She lay down on her towel and pressed her face into her arms.

"Aren't you going to take off your shorts?" Karen asked.

"I like her cut-offs," Robyn said. "They're cool."

Frankie's stomach roiled. She squeezed her bum; a small burst of gas escaped. It was silent, but Frankie could smell the fart's pungent aftermath.

She jumped up and grabbed her towel. "I forgot I'm supposed to be home early."

Robyn followed her, "You said your dad said yes."

"But I forgot and I have to go."

"Somebody farted," Lisa said.

"Why do you have to go?" Robyn was close to tears.

"I'm sorry," Frankie said. She hurried out of the yard.

"Gross!" Karen squealed.

"Shut up," Frankie heard Robyn say as she left the yard.

"Robyn!" Mrs. Oliver snapped. "I'll have you remember your manners."

Frankie hurried toward her bike. On the bottom stair, a blue and white book, *The Guide Handbook*, was face down against the step. Frankie picked it up; it was open to chapter ten, with the words *Good Grooming* in large bold letters.

She heard Robyn and her mother's raised voices. Frankie glanced around but saw no one. She clutched *The Guide Handbook*, hopped on her bike and pedalled away from Robyn's big house and the beautiful man-made lake with its man-made waterfall and tiny island. She had never seen anything so nice.

Law Awareness

 At the Oliver family dinner table, Robyn picked quietly at her casserole. Her father ate with gusto. Mrs. Oliver ate a salad.

"Somebody's quiet," Robyn's dad observed.

"Somebody's sulking," her mom said.

"Karen and Lisa were mean," Robyn said.

"Oh, come now," Gloria Oliver waved her hand, "they were just being girls."

"I hate them," Robyn said.

"Well you'd better get used to them," Gloria snapped. "You'll be seeing a lot of them once the new school year starts."

"I want to go to Frankie's school."

"You are not going to Catholic school!"

"Why not?"

Gloria lit a cigarette, "Ken, help me out, would you?"

"Well, honey," Ken Oliver said. "For starters, we're not Catholic."

Gloria shook her finger. "For starters." She held up a second finger. "The girl lives in a trailer court, for God's sake!" And then a third finger. "She was absolutely filthy."

"She was not!" Robyn cried.

Gloria raised her eyebrows.

"Her mom died," Robyn said.

"All the more reason to stay away," said Gloria. "A single father? I don't think so."

"Why are you being so mean?"

"I'll thank you to show me some respect, young lady. And trust that I know what's best for you. I don't want you seeing that girl anymore."

"Daddy!" Robyn clasped her hands together, imploring her father.

He shook his head. "Why do you want to be playing with someone from a trailer court when you could be on the lake here, with girls you're going to be going to school with?"

"Precisely," Gloria said. "You've barely set foot in the lake."

"Because I've been working on my stalking badge!"

"You haven't even managed your backyard camping badge," Gloria said.

"Stalking what?" Ken asked.

"Gophers."

"Rodents?" Gloria brought her fingers to her forehead and closed her eyes. "Give me patience." She looked at Robyn. "If you want to earn your stalking badge then I suggest you go with you father in the fall, when he goes duck hunting."

"Oh, I don't know about that," Ken said.

"I hate ducks," Robyn said.

"Well, you're not stalking a bloody gopher," Gloria said. "Not while I'm captain."

"You're not captain, you're lieutenant," Robyn said.

"Don't you sass me," Gloria said. She looked at her husband. "Look at the trouble that girl is causing."

"Your mother is right," Ken said.

Robyn started to cry.

"That's enough," Gloria said. "Finish your dinner."

"I'm not hungry." Robyn brushed a tear from her cheek.

"There'll be nothing for you to eat later on," Gloria snapped.

"We're just looking out for you, darling," Ken said.

Robyn pushed away from the table, ran up the short flight of stairs to her room and slammed the door.

Gloria rubbed her cigarette into the ashtray then stood up. "I'm going to make a gin and tonic," she said. "Would you like one?"

"A stiff one," Ken said with a mouth full of food.

Second Class

Frankie had the whole trailer to herself but lay in Bernie's bunk. She could still smell Bernie's shampoo on the pillow.

Yesterday was the second worst day of her whole life.

Yesterday, when they met up, Robyn was crying her head off. She was only allowed to stay long enough to say goodbye. Frankie flipped onto her belly, shame snapping through her. Robyn's parents didn't like Frankie because her mom was dead. Robyn's parents didn't like Frankie because she was scruffy.

"But I never even met your dad," Frankie said to Robyn.

"I know, but he does whatever she tells him to," Robyn sobbed.

Robyn was perched on her knees like she was praying, her hands clasped in front of her chest.

"I don't even care if I get dirty," she said. She lay down and rested her head in Frankie's lap. Robyn wiped the snot from her nose with her hand and smeared it across the bum of her shorts. "She can drop dead."

"Don't say that," Frankie said.

"I mean it," Robyn wept. Her braids were loose; her shorts were shiny with snot and her sneakers were scuffed with dirt. Her mom was going to be mad.

Frankie stroked Robyn's hair and hushed her. Robyn's mom was making her stay on their street for the rest of the summer.

"I have to go," Robyn whispered.

The two girls hugged.

"Blood sisters," Robyn said.

Frankie nodded.

Robyn ran until she was nearly out of sight then she turned back and held up her hand like a benediction. Frankie did the same then watched as Robyn ran out of sight.

"What the hell happened to you?" Bernadette said when Frankie got home. And after Frankie told her, Bernadette said that Robyn's mom was a fucking bitch and she made Frankie a brown sugar sandwich.

"You've got to be tough now, Frankie." She pulled Frances onto her lap and hugged her. "I'm sorry, kid. It's been such a lousy summer."

Frankie pressed her face into Bernadette's pillow. She wouldn't even have to hide that she'd been down here in the forbidden zone because Bernie wasn't coming back, because she had to give her baby away because it was a sin to have a baby unless you were married. But there were married people who couldn't have babies and who would take Bernie's baby, so why was Bern even a sinner then? God was stupid if He couldn't see she was doing something nice for those people.

"You're stupid," Frankie said to God. "And I don't believe in you anymore. And that is that."

Because they had to stick together. If Bernadette was a sinner then Frankie was going to be a sinner, too.

Tenderfoot

 Bernadette was on the Greyhound, somewhere east of Medicine Hat. It was dark outside and the bus was quiet. Someone a few rows behind her lit up a smoke; its aroma drifted toward Bernadette and made her long for a cigarette of her own. The old lady next to her was sleeping, her head resting on Bernadette's shoulder.

Earlier in the evening, when she'd said goodbye, Frankie began to cry. Bernadette promised that she would write lots of letters. Jimmy stood behind Frankie, pulling at his mouth. He passed Bernadette fifty bucks and told her to make it last. What was she going to spend money on anyways? The most she could stomach was toast, crackers and weak tea.

The smoker behind her nearly coughed up a lung, a wet and wheezy expectoration that caused everyone around Bernadette to shift position, except for the old lady. Well, whatever else was going to happen, at least she was out of that shithole of a trailer court. Poor Frankie still had years left in that dump. Bernadette stared out the window. It was too dark to see much now, just the silhouette of a pumpjack, dipping its mechanical head into a farmer's field, illuminated by the lights of an oncoming car.

Acknowledgements

Thank you to Kevin Allen, who runs calgaryqueerhistory.ca, for the background information provided from Calgary Gay History Project's archives and for the connections with Nancy and Leslie. Thank you to Nancy Miller, who was very helpful in recalling early eighties queer Calgary. And thank you to Leslie Wilkins for the spur-of-the-moment chat recalling the Womyn's Collective and Lesbian Information Line, which was such a great service to so many Calgary women back in the day – so much was clarified for me in our short conversation. Thank you to Sharon Stevens, who has kept and gathered historical Calgary information and passed it on to me like a champ. A shout-out to my brother Mike for helping me get the beer brands right and for consultation on the kind of work a man like Jimmy Murray might have done. And a big thank you to Olga Filina, who carefully read an earlier draft of this novel and provided me with some welcome insights for future drafts.

I have a lifetime of gratitude to my cousin John Lefebvre, who financially supported me for a decade. I cannot overstate the positive, life-changing effect of such radical support.

To my Cullen clan, I cherish the big, boisterous foundation of your companionship. What an excellent trip to grow up with a bunch like you. And thank you as well to my LeBlanc family. I am so grateful to have remained within your circle.

I am blessed by the life-sustaining friendships of my Calgary squad, Sharon, Sharron, Kathy, Joni, Laura, Lizzie, Melanie, Jodie and Elizabeth.

Ayelet, Becky, Eufemia, Kathy, Kilby and Leesa, your friendship, inspiration, and writing and words talk also sustain.

Thanks to my Book City pals for a great few years of work and friendship.

Thank you to Paul Vermeersch, Noelle Allen, Ashley Hisson and the rest of the Wolsak and Wynn team. Also to Michel Vrana for his amazing book design.

Helen, Luke and Claire, you make my life so much better.

I would like to thank the Girl Guides of Canada for access to their archives, and a special thank you to Catherine Miller-Mort, who gave me a copy of *The Guide Handbook* to keep.

And last, but not least, I am very grateful to the Ontario Arts Council for financial support during the writing of this book.

Nancy Jo Cullen is the fourth recipient of the Writers' Trust Dayne Ogilvie Prize for LGBT Emerging Writers. She holds an MFA in Creative Writing from the University of Guelph-Humber and her short story collection, *Canary*, was the winner of the 2012 Metcalf-Rooke Award. Her poetry has been shortlisted for the Gerald Lampert Memorial Award, the Writers' Guild of Alberta's Stephan G. Stephansson Award and the City of Calgary W.O. Mitchell Book Prize. She lived in Calgary for over two decades and still returns regularly to connect with family and friends. She now lives in Kingston, Canada.